Courteous, courageous and commanding—
these heroes lay it all on the line for the
people they love in more than fifty stories about
loyalty, bravery and romance.
Don't miss a single one!

MEN
in
UNIFORM

USA TODAY Bestselling Author

JILL
SHALVIS

SERVING UP TROUBLE

Silhouette Books

Published by Silhouette Books
America's Publisher of Contemporary Romance

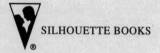 SILHOUETTE BOOKS

Recycling programs
for this product may
not exist in your area.

ISBN-13: 978-0-373-36280-6

SERVING UP TROUBLE

Visit Silhouette Books at www.eHarlequin.com

Printed in U.S.A.

JILL SHALVIS

USA TODAY bestselling and award-winning Jill Shalvis is the author of more than fifty romance novels, including a series with firefighter heroes for Harlequin Books. The three-time RITA® Award nominee and three-time National Readers' Choice winner makes her home near Lake Tahoe. Visit her Web site at www.jillshalvis.com for a complete book list and daily blog.

Chapter 1

She'd always been happy enough. Well, if not happy exactly, then…content. But deep down, Angie Rivers knew something was missing from her life; she just couldn't put her finger on it. Why should she, when she had a fine job, a fine apartment and fine friends.

Fine everything, really—unless she thought about it too hard, as she sometimes tended to do.

In any case, the niggling remained a mystery.

Until Monday.

By the time her break came she was already tired from waiting tables, but she had to get to the bank. She'd written her rent check, along with a check for what could be termed a luxury item—an artist's easel. Her first and, as a budding painter, she was very excited about it.

Racing down the block in the warm California sunshine, she dodged bikers, in-line skaters, scooters…it was Monday, for God's sake. Why weren't people working?

If she didn't have to work, what would she do? What a delightful dilemma to face. She'd kill herself if she strapped on a pair of skates, but…a day to sit in the park and sketch? An entire day to stand in front of her new easel and paint? Mmm, nice fantasy.

Inside the bank, she hit the midmorning crowd. And a very long line. With a sigh, Angie pushed up her glasses and looked around at the people waiting ahead of her. As was usual for this upscale area of South Pasadena, everyone was dressed for success. Even the bank tellers.

She tugged at the skirt of her waitress uniform, knowing few would understand that she did love her job, hard as it was. There hadn't been money for college when she'd graduated high school seven years ago, despite her parents' hopes and dreams of her becoming a doctor or lawyer.

Sweet, but unrealistic. Angie hadn't been the best high school student, hadn't played sports or had a good hobby, either, mostly because she'd always worked to help her parents make ends meet. She hadn't minded, though sometimes she wished they'd really see her, *her,* Angie Rivers, and not just what they dreamed Angie Rivers to be.

Disturbingly enough, her parents' expectations only seemed to get more unrealistic the older they became. Why hadn't she become successful? Rich? Well connected?

Married with brilliant children?

She didn't like to admit that she'd dug in her heels and purposely become the antithesis of their out-of-reach expectations. But that's what she'd done.

She had goals for herself—they just didn't match anyone else's. She wanted to paint. There wasn't a whole heck of a lot of money in that, unless she found some superb talent from deep within. Oh, and she'd also have to die, as most artists made all their money posthumously.

The bank line she'd chosen still hadn't budged, and there she stood, with only seven minutes left on her break. Craning her neck, she saw an older woman at the counter, doling out change to the teller. One coin at a time.

Behind her was every mother's nightmare. A young punk, wiry and dressed for a ghetto fashion show, paced edgily, muttering to himself. He looked like a simmering pot ready to explode.

The man in front of her had a swagger. A sort of I'm-God's-gift-to-women swagger. Angie could easily overlook his cheap, light blue suit and tacky tie as she appreciated—and remembered with vivid clarity—the pain of never having the in clothes.

She was still feeling that pain.

What she couldn't ignore was the way he invaded her space and kept winking at her.

"Come here often?" he actually asked her, brushing his shoulder against hers.

She didn't answer, hoping he'd give up if she didn't encourage him. His hair had been slicked back with enough gel to grease a pig. His breath was hot and smelled like tuna.

"Is the sun shining?" he wondered. "Because I can't see anything but stars when I look at you."

Angie tried a vague smile—*why was the line still moving so slowly?*—and turned her back to him.

With or without the tuna breath and bad pickup line, she wasn't much interested in men. Her ex-fiancé Tony had been no better than her own parents when it came to seeing her, understanding her, and she was tired of that, thank you very much.

She was who she was. A great waitress. A

wanna-be artist. She was fine, darn them all. Fine just as she was.

She peered behind her and saw that Mr. Edgy had gotten worse. His fists were clenched, his jaw tight. Pure fire and hatred sprang from his eyes, and though she couldn't understand his mutterings, the tone was universal.

And dangerous.

Angie had heard of highway rage, but this waiting-in-a-terminally-slow-line rage was new to her, and a little scary. Shivering, she turned sideways, feeling sandwiched by desperation.

In the next line over stood another man, and this one looked as impatient as she felt. Arms crossed, feet tapping, mouth turned downward in a frown, he embodied the man on the move. Only he was the most heart-stopping man on the move she'd ever seen.

He looked out of place. Not because he was tall, leanly muscular, and gorgeous to boot. Not because he'd disregarded the up-and-comer Southern California look for a simple blue T-shirt tucked into perfectly soft and faded 501s. It was that he made everyone around him look as if they were playing dress-up.

He scowled at his own unmoving line, all testosterone and barely contained power as his searing light brown gaze scanned the large, hustling bank.

Just looking at him made Angie felt a little breathless. She stood up taller, wondering what he thought when he looked at her. She knew what she thought when she looked at him. *Whoa,* baby.

He had sun-kissed hair cut short to his head. His rugged, athletic physique said he could have graced any men's magazine he wanted, and he didn't so much as give Angie a cursory glance when his eyes carefully and purposely surveyed the room.

Check your ego at the door, Angie.

The bank clerk called for the next customer with all the cheer of a woman facing a bikini wax. Mr. Tacky Suit swaggered up there while Angie willed the line to keep moving.

Two minutes left on her break.

One minute.

Then—finally—it was her turn. With a sigh of relief, she moved across the tile floor toward the distracted-looking teller. The woman had a beehive hairstyle that looked as if maybe she'd worn it for the past fifty years, and fuchsia-pink lipstick. She glared at Angie as if it were her fault she had to deal with slime buckets in light blue suits.

Later, Angie would marvel at how quickly it all seemed to happen, but for now, time shifted into slow motion. One minute she was glancing at her watch and handing over her signed check, and the next, Mr. Edgy had grabbed her arm from behind.

"Hey—" she started, annoyed, only to swallow the words when the tip of a knife appeared in front of her eyes before settling against her neck.

"Give me all the money in your drawer," he said to the startled teller while still holding on to Angie. "And don't even *think* about the panic button."

Amazingly enough, as Angie was turned in the robber's arms so that he had a better grasp on her, everyone had froze on the spot. Even Mr. Knock-Me-Over-Magnificent, whose big body had gone tense and battle ready, didn't make a move.

"Do it, lady," the man growled at the teller, who let out a little cry and froze like a deer caught in the headlights.

Angie had a moment to feel badly she'd mentally poked fun at the woman's choice of lipstick color before she was rudely whipped forward again. Mr. Edgy stared down at her with a look of blatant hatred, and she took a terrified breath that ended in a little squeak. Fear iced her veins so that her ears rang, making it difficult to hear anything other than the echo of her own blood racing.

"You'll be my ticket outta here." The knife

flashed beneath her nose again, making her glasses slip too low. "Got it?"

A response didn't seem to be required, so she closed her eyes, realizing now was a heck of a time to suddenly understand what was wrong with her life—it was *boring!* She lived her life so purposely staidly to avoid the parents' hopes and dreams that it had become utterly…unnecessary.

"Move and you die," the punk said with enough fury in his voice that Angie believed every word. "Scream and you die. *Breathe* and you die."

Okay, she got it. She was pretty much dead.

The teller moaned in distress, and her fingers attempted to work the drawer in front of her, but she couldn't quite seem to manage it. Angie wanted to scream at her.

"Move it," the guy holding her muttered to the shaking woman.

The teller stared at him blankly and he yelled it again. "Money! *Now!*" For emphasis he shook Angie, hard.

She couldn't contain the helpless whimper that was ripped from her throat. Her sweater tore from her shoulder. Her glasses slipped off her nose, but she couldn't catch them because he held her so tight. She heard them hit the floor.

Without them, her vision blurred. Her world

became reduced to the knife against her throat. The cold steel of the knife dug into her skin. The arm that held her imprisoned was amazingly strong and her knees wobbled as her life flashed before her eyes.

Unnecessary.

Oh, yes, *that's* what the niggling had been. Her life had been too unnecessary. Anyone could have lived it. That it was because she'd tried so hard to break free from those expectations of her didn't make her feel any better. A wasted life was a wasted life.

She needed more time. She needed another chance. She wouldn't waste anything this time!

Her heart drummed. She broke out into a sweat. As if from a mile away, she could hear the teller fumble at her drawer with clumsy fingers, but it must not have opened, because the man holding her swore lividly beneath his breath and shook her again, so hard this time that she cried out more loudly.

"Shut up." His grip tightened, and Angie cringed, biting her tongue, waiting for the searing pain she figured would accompany a deep knife wound.

"Money," he demanded of the teller. "Give me the money!"

"I'm trying!"

It wasn't going to happen, Angie realized blindly. He'd petrified the poor teller so thoroughly that the woman didn't have a chance in hell of opening the drawer, not with those violently shaking fingers, not to mention the shock that had already set in, making her eyes two huge blurry orbs of panic.

Angie was going to die, right here, right now, and all because of bad timing. If she hadn't written the rent check, if she hadn't forgotten to come to the bank yesterday, if, if, if…she could think of a thousand of them.

Standing there, as good as a blind mouse, her sense of absurdity took over. Why else would she think about her apartment, and the plants that would die without her?

And, oh God, she was wearing underwear with a rip in the elastic. Her mother had warned her about that, hadn't she, about getting in an accident with torn panties? Now everyone in the hospital would know.

If she even made it to a hospital.

Her parents would be contacted and told the truth. Their daughter had died before becoming someone. Anyone. And she'd died in old underwear.

It would kill them.

A shot rang out, and Angie automatically jerked.

Then something slammed into her captor, hard enough to loosen his hold on her. The momentum sent her to her knees with a bone-jarring crunch.

Someone screamed.

And screamed.

Pandemonium seemed to strike and Angie lifted her head, squinting like crazy, but it was no use—everything was out of focus.

She could hear and feel though, so that when she was scooped up against a warm, hard chest, her hair shoved out of her eyes by a big, callused palm, she somehow instinctively knew who had her.

Mr. Knock-Me-Over-Magnificent.

Her hero.

"Are you all right?" Sam O'Brien demanded.

When the woman's huge eyes just blinked up at him, he swore to himself. Heart thudding, he tipped her head back, his fingers running over her neck, looking for the wound as he went cold inside.

Amazingly enough, he found nothing but a slight scratch, and lots of warm, creamy skin with soft, satiny light brown hair that had escaped its confines.

"You okay?" he pressed, needing to hear her, his voice rough with concern and rushing adrenaline.

Again she blinked those big, dark brown eyes,

then squinted. "I...can't see very well. Everything is fuzzy."

His heart wedged in his throat. Had she hit her head? Damn it, despite everything, had she gotten hurt?

It had been every off-duty cop's greatest nightmare as he'd stood in line watching the attempted robbery take place. He'd had no backup, no radio, nothing but the comforting weight of his own gun at his back.

And too many possible victims to count.

He'd been forced to wait until the punk with the knife had turned away, knowing if he moved too soon the woman would die right in front of his eyes.

So he'd held his breath while she'd been cruelly shaken and manhandled, biding his time so that he didn't get her killed.

Finally he'd had his moment and he'd fired.

The bad guy was now bleeding, unconscious on the floor, and this wide-eyed beauty in his arms appeared to be going into shock.

"Get an ambulance," he barked to the growing crowd, but he could hear the siren in the distance. "Good. Okay," he said, squeezing the woman's arm. "They're on their way, you're going to be fine."

"I'm not hurt. I just can't see well. Is he... dead?"

Sam glanced over, saw the chest rising and falling on the perp. "No."

Using Sam's shoulder for leverage, she sat up and pushed at the hair falling in her face. She reached down to pull at her torn sweater, then patted her hands on the floor, searching while still wrapped securely in his embrace.

"What are you doing?"

"I need my glasses."

Sam glanced around him as police stormed the building. The customers seemed to be still shell-shocked and only started moving when the police ordered them to walk single file out of the bank.

"Do you see them?" she asked, her voice full of worry that was probably not related in the slightest to her lost glasses, but more to shock.

Inches away, next to the body sprawled out and now moaning as he was being worked on by para-medics who just arrived, were the glasses.

Crushed.

She let out a soft sigh when he handed them to her, then she leaned back to rest against his strong, sturdy frame. "This is turning out to be a really bad day," she said, looking calm, *too* calm. In-shock calm.

"You were nearly killed." He remained sitting on the floor, the fragile beauty in his arms and gestured to a paramedic, who held up a finger to indicate he'd be right there. "It's okay to fall apart a little."

"I don't fall apart." And yet her voice wobbled in the growing din around them. "My glasses…"

"Can be replaced. Your life sure as hell can't."

"Yes. Yes, you're right. You saved my life. I can't thank you enough for what you did."

"It's okay," he said, not giving a damn about a thank-you.

"But I have no idea what would have happened if you hadn't jumped right in. You were wonderful, so brave."

Obviously she was completely unaware he was a cop and, as such, paid to be brave.

"In fact, let me—" She shifted against him and fumbled for her purse, which by some miracle was still hanging off her arm. "I want to give you…"

Was she for real? She wanted to *pay* him?

But the tremor that racked her was very real and she went suddenly, absolutely still. "I'm sorry," she whispered, clutching her purse to her chest with a heartbreaking expression. In her fist she held something that she smoothed out.

A paycheck for 198.00 made out to Angie Rivers.

"I never got to make my deposit." She squinted at it. "I have my tips, but they're not much."

She looked as though maybe she didn't *ever* have much, but he held his tongue as an unwelcome wave of emotion washed over him.

He hated this, he really did. All he'd wanted to do was to shift some money to his checking account, then head over to his partner and best friend Luke's house for pizza and beer.

Instead he'd stopped a bank robbery, and now he sat on the floor, holding the most amazing woman, feeling everything he'd trained himself not to feel.

Finally the paramedics descended on them, taking the still shell-shocked woman from his arms. Sam rose to his feet, thankful to be free of the victim.

Even if his arms felt empty.

He had no idea why he followed her. She was sweetly arguing with the medics that she was fine, that she needed to hurry up and deposit her check and get back to work, she had tables to wait.

The on-duty officers stopped her. They needed her statement, which she gave. Then it was his turn, and they pulled him aside from where he'd been standing, watching over her.

When it was done, in front of all the witnesses and far too many bloodsucking reporters that had come out of the woodworks, Angie reached out for him and hugged him. "I just wanted to thank you again," she said, pulling him close, nearly squeezing the very life out of him with her nervous, awkward embrace.

His arms wrapped around her before he could stop himself, and when she placed a loud, smacking kiss on his cheek, he sucked in a hard breath, shocked. He, Sam O'Brien, shrewd detective and hardened, cynical cop, who was never shocked by anything.

She swiped at what he could only assume was lip gloss, which smelled like a bowl of peaches and cream. "Sorry," she whispered, then beamed at him, her fingers still on his cheek, and because she was so close, he couldn't help but feel her fingers tremble, see her smile wobble.

Ah, hell. "You're not okay."

"Yes, I am. Really." But her smile was definitely shaky around the edges. "You were my hero today. I wish I could say I hadn't needed one, but I did, and thank God you were here. I only hope someday

I can somehow return the favor and do something this big for you."

Before he could so much as blink, she was walking away.

Only to be mobbed by the press.

Sam watched them deluge her with questions, shoving their microphones in her face.

Just walk away, he told himself.

But Angie's expression went from shock to lost, and he let out one pithy oath before striding over there. "Go," he said into her ear, his hand at the small of her back, giving her a little push. "I'll hold them off."

That won him a smile that stopped him in his tracks.

For some reason—it couldn't be anything as simple as her smile—Sam stood there long after she'd fled. Long enough to get him his own mob of reporters.

As a rule, he really hated the press. Most cops did. His dad had. It was one of those things he remembered about him. That, and how much his dad had loved everything else about being a cop. One of Sam's first memories was of standing in front of the mirror, wearing his father's police hat and holding up his fingers in a solemn vow to serve and protect.

He'd been four.

His conviction had held steadfast, even after his father had been killed in the line of duty during a routine traffic incident gone awry that same year.

So while Sam stood there, being thanked for his quick reactions, being hailed a hero, he felt only a bone-deep weariness.

He wasn't a hero, not even close. He was just doing his job.

When Sam finally made it home to his modest, quiet condo, he realized he'd forgotten to go to Luke's.

He'd forgotten the beer, the pizza.

He'd forgotten every damn thing, which was very unlike him.

To add to the insult, he dreamed about soft, creamy, satiny skin, and chocolate-brown eyes. Dreamed about her lithe yet curvy body and how it had felt against his. Dreamed about her voice, the intoxicating mix of sweet innocence and wild sexiness.

Dreamed about the woman to whom it all belonged.

Angie Rivers.

Chapter 2

When Angie woke up the next morning, every single light in her apartment was glaring. Wincing, she rolled over and hid her eyes from the brightness she'd used to ward off her silly fears during the night.

So she'd nearly been killed. So what? She'd survived, hadn't she? And the bad guy had been caught, so she didn't really need to send her electric bill through the roof.

But she'd probably do the same tonight.

She really wished she'd somehow managed to save herself yesterday. Then she'd have felt stronger during the night. Invincible.

Maybe next time.

Getting up, putting on an old pair of glasses to replace the broken ones, she took comfort in her small, cozy and slightly messy apartment. *Small* and *cozy* being nice words for what was really postage-stamp sized.

But cluttered or not, it was clean, it was her home, and she refused to let anyone frighten her here.

"There. Take that, monsters. I'm not frightened."

In the bathroom, she gave herself a good, long, hard look in the mirror. She appeared to be the same as yesterday, average height, average body, average everything.

But she wasn't the same, not at all, and wouldn't be ever again. "You know what? No more simply existing," she told her reflection. "That's not good enough for you."

With that small but effective pep talk, she went into the kitchen and had her usual breakfast of champions—a bagel that had more cream cheese than bagel.

A woman needed her protein.

By the time she left for work, she'd taken several phone calls from her worried parents and friends, wanting to make sure she was okay. And mostly, she was.

But what had happened to her yesterday had been a sign. A change-her-life kind of sign. A become-a-new-woman sign.

She knew this, and didn't plan on wasting it. She'd been reminded—violently—how fast it could all end. And she wasn't ready for an end, not by a long shot.

In light of that, she pulled out the local junior college application she'd received in the mail last month. Classes were due to start this week, a coincidence she'd take as another sign. She might love painting, but she couldn't support herself that way. Time to find something she could do with her love of the arts that she could make a living at.

Without giving herself a chance to talk herself out of it, she filled in the required forms, wrote a check for late registration and stuffed them into her pocket to drop off on her way to work.

It felt…incredible. And she didn't understand why it had taken her so long to do it, why she hadn't seen what she'd needed to do a long time ago.

The phone rang again, and Angie answered with an indulgent laugh, feeling better, wondering which of her friends had felt the need to check up on her this time.

"Angie Rivers?"

The laugh backed up in her throat. She instantly

recognized that low, deep, slightly husky voice. She had a feeling a hundred years could go by and she'd *still* recognize it.

That voice had been the first she'd heard after her terrifying ordeal yesterday. That voice had gone along with warm, strong arms and eyes filled with rage and concern, for her, in a way a man's never had before.

That voice liquefied her bones.

With her spare glasses perched on her nose, she glanced at the front page of the newspaper sitting on her table, a page on which both she and Sam O'Brien—decorated, revered, respected detective—were splashed across.

"Yes, this is Angie," she said, having to sit down because suddenly she was made of Jell-O, with no bones in her entire body.

"This is Sam O'Brien, from yesterday—"

"I know." She was still looking at the picture of the two of them on the floor of the bank in the aftermath of the attempted robbery. She'd already inhaled every little tidbit about what had happened.

About Sam.

The newspaper didn't say he was tall, with wheat-colored, sun-bleached hair cut short to his head, which only emphasized his sharp, light brown eyes. It also failed to mention he was built with a rugged, athletic physique that revved her hormones, but then again, the reporter hadn't been held in his warm, strong, wonderful arms.

Angie had.

She sighed, then shook her head. She had a plan, and a man did not fit into it. Never had, in fact, though she'd tried. She just didn't seem to have what it took to please one—not the drive, not the easy sensuality so many other women had.

So she'd given up.

Until yesterday, that is, when she'd come far too close to death. Now she knew she would never give up on anything, not ever again.

Life had to be lived, mistakes and all.

"We need you to come down to the station," he said. "We have some more questions. Do you need a car sent for you?"

A ride in a squad car down to the station. An adventure she could really do without, if she had a choice. "That's not necessary. I'll…stop by."

"Okay, then."

He was going to hang up now. And though she couldn't explain it, she wasn't ready to let go, to stop hearing him. She'd like to be able to attribute it to lingering shock or fear, but she knew better.

Nothing about his voice reminded her of shock

or fear. Instead it invoked visions of things she'd never shared with anyone but had always fantasized about; lying in bed on a Sunday morning sharing the funny section of the paper, late-night forays into the freezer for a tub of ice cream that they'd feed to each other with one spoon, or better yet just eat off their bodies, phone calls during the day just to hear each other… "Are you the investigating officer then?" she asked. *Subtle, Ang.*

"No, that would be Detective Owens. He'll be questioning you."

But Sam had called her himself. Maybe he was dreaming of the comics and ice cream, too. Maybe he yearned and ached and burned for things he couldn't quite put into words but knew he wanted.

With her.

"Owens asked me to call," he clarified.

Which pretty much dispelled both the fantasy and any lingering hope that somehow this strange, inexplicable attraction was two-sided.

"Sometimes," he continued, "in traumatic events like this, a familiar voice helps."

Was that what all this emotion crowding her chest was about? Because he was familiar? Because he'd been her hero in a terrible incident?

That was pathetic.

Even more so because he clearly felt none of

what she'd allowed herself to feel. "I see," she said, grateful that at least he couldn't see her. "Well… thank you."

"No problem."

Wait. She wanted to tell him how much his actions yesterday had meant. How much she'd learned about herself since. How—

Click.

Dial tone.

With a little sigh, Angie had to laugh. She set the phone down and decided to stick with reality. *Her* reality.

Which at the moment, she thought, glancing at her clock, meant work.

But later, she promised the new easel standing in her living room, later she'd paint. Just because she could.

Sam spent the morning chasing dead ends, trying to crack the identity-theft ring that had already spent over a million dollars in stolen credit in the past calendar year alone.

Back in his office, he collapsed in frustration at his desk before a commotion outside the door caught his attention. He tried to ignore it, but wasn't lucky enough for that.

A shadow crossed his desk. "Well, if it isn't our local hero."

Sam glanced up at his partner, who until a second ago had also been his best friend, and scowled. Most people went running from that fierce, foreboding glare, or at least walked quickly away.

Not Luke Sorrintino. He was dark-haired, darker-skinned and full-blooded Italian, and he didn't scare easily. While he was only medium build to Sam's tall, broader one, he was probably the toughest man Sam knew, and he rarely smiled.

But he was smiling now, broadly.

"What do you want?" Sam asked, already wary.

"Two things. First…" He tossed down the morning paper.

Front page, dead center. Sam on his knees on the floor of the bank, with a beautiful, disheveled woman in his arms, staring up at him with huge, grateful eyes.

Angie.

God, she looked so small, so defenseless. So absolutely, heart-wrenchingly vulnerable. Her sweater hung off one shoulder, revealing soft skin, which according to the color photo, had already started to bruise from her captor's cruel grip.

Sam's jaw went tight. A headache kicked in. She'd gotten hurt after all.

"You seem pretty…involved," Luke noted.

Sam's eyes honed in on his face in the picture. Sure enough, he wasn't just holding her, he was *holding* her, cradling her against his chest, one hand spread over her exposed throat. His expression was intense to say the least, and zeroed in one-hundred percent on Angie's upturned face.

It looked startlingly intimate, and if he didn't know that he'd been concerned only with making sure she hadn't been cut by the punk's knife, that she was looking at him like that only because she could hardly see…damn. Take away the bank setting, take away the fact that there was a bleeding criminal on the floor behind them, and they could have been… lovers.

"Interesting," Luke said.

Sam eyed his friend. The two of them had been through a lot together. High school. The academy. Being rookies. They'd been through family and wives unable, or unwilling, to handle the demands of their jobs.

Death and mayhem. They'd seen or done it all.

Were *still* seeing and doing it all.

"Oh, I almost forgot." Luke actually kept

grinning, which really made Sam pause. "There's a delivery for you."

"Yeah? So bring it in."

"Delivery woman insists on giving it to you herself."

Delivery *woman?*

With a long, warning look to Luke, Sam rose to his feet and came to the door of his office. He wasn't pleased to see a small crowd of cops who plainly had nothing better to do than stand around and smile stupidly.

In the center of the group was a *huge* bouquet of wildflowers sprouting three feet wide out of a basket. He couldn't see the face of the person behind it, only that she was wearing sandals, with bright pink polished toenails and a dainty little gold toe-ring.

Then from behind the basket peeked a smiling face.

Angie.

Around him there were hushed whispers and more than a few teeters and muffled laughter.

Sam ignored them to stare at her in disbelief. Flowers. Lord, she'd brought flowers to the toughest, meanest cop in the precinct.

He'd never live it down.

"I've brought a thank-you for yesterday," she said

in a sweet, musical voice that somehow had him stepping from his office doorway toward her.

He managed to stop himself a few feet away, very aware of their audience. "You already thanked me."

If his gruffness startled her, as it tended to do to most everyone else, she didn't show it. Her smile brightened even more, if that was possible, and she lifted a shoulder. "Truth is, Detective O'Brien, I could never thank you enough. You've given me more than you could ever know."

He didn't want her gratitude. What he *did* want couldn't be said in polite company.

She peered into his small, none-too-tidy office. "Besides, it looks as though you might be able to use some color in that room. How do you work in there? It's dark as a tomb."

Sam found himself staring at her petite form as she walked past him and into his office as if she owned the place. Her nicely rounded bottom sashayed beneath her sundress, as she marched right to his overcrowded desk.

"Wait—" No use, she was already making room, stacking piles of carefully sorted paperwork together—negating hours of work—and setting the basket down.

Then she moved to the window and reached for the shades.

"No—" He hated having all that bright sunshine pouring in over his shoulder when he was concentrating. "Don't open—"

Too late.

She yanked the string, throwing light into the room. "There. That's so much better, isn't it?" She tossed her hair out of her eyes—hair that he couldn't help but notice was a million different colors, like a doe's coat, and smelled even better than the flowers she'd just settled.

She smiled at him. "This is really a bad color for your office walls. Drab gray. It's not at all conducive to happy work patterns."

He'd never even noticed what color the walls were, and didn't care to now. Nor was he thrilled about noticing her hair color.

He had work to do.

"You know, I always had the secret fantasy of going through the police academy," she said wistfully, looking around. "I had this dream of rounding up all the bad guys and putting them behind bars."

The thought of this far too cheerful, happy, bouncy, flowers-carrying woman going through the academy brought a fine sweat to Sam's brow. "You wouldn't like it," he said quickly.

"Oh, I think I would. Well, except for the shooting part." She shivered. "I'm not crazy about weapons." Her smile faded and a shadow flickered across her face. "Give me a paintbrush any day."

Sam knew she was remembering yesterday, having a flashback to when she'd had the blade of a knife pressed against her slim neck. Damn it, he didn't want to know this. Didn't want to know how traumatized she was, or see how badly she was bruised. He searched her with his gaze, but couldn't see a thing with her halter-top sundress that covered her to the throat. "Are you okay?"

"Oh, yes. Thanks to you."

She was as small as he remembered, barely coming up to his shoulder. But where had all her defenseless vulnerability of yesterday gone? She looked totally, utterly capable of anything, especially ruining his day.

"You found a spare pair of glasses," he heard himself say inanely, gesturing to the frames she wore.

"They're ancient—oops." She bit her lower lip to hold back a smile. "Probably shouldn't tell that to a police officer. I could get a ticket for driving with an old prescription, right?"

He was relieved to discover she hadn't just purchased the thick, blue-rimmed, almost horn-shaped glasses. He felt an odd pang at the knowledge she probably couldn't afford a brand-new pair. He wondered if the bank wouldn't cover the cost for her, and opened his mouth to suggest something to that effect when the curious whispers behind him registered.

He whirled to the doorway, and found Luke and two rookies leaning in his door, unabashedly eavesdropping.

"Need something to do?" he inquired. At his cold voice, the rookies instantly scattered.

Luke just grinned before slowly straightening and walking away.

Angie was staring at him with those huge brown eyes. "Wow," she said, impressed. "That was a pretty scary cop voice. Really fierce. Do you use that on criminals to make them confess?"

Yeah, or on unwelcome guests to get them to leave. But he found he didn't have quite the heart to say it. A surprise, and it only worsened his mood.

He really had a ton of work to do. He wanted— *needed*—to crack his priority case, and soon, as the suspects were probably right this minute stealing mail or trash, racking up more uncollectible debt by the minute.

"You know," Angie said, sizing up his office, the wheels visibly turning in her head. "You could really use a paint job on these walls."

"A paint job," he repeated slowly.

"Maybe pink? It would most definitely help ease your tension."

Oh yeah, that's what he needed. Pink walls. "I'm not tense."

She raised her brow so high it disappeared into her bangs. "Really? Then why is your jaw all tight and bunchy?"

"It's not."

"I can see the muscle jumping."

It jumped some more. "I'm fine."

"If this is normal for you, you must go home with a heck of a neck ache. Come here and sit down. I'll rub it for you."

He actually backed up. "I said I'm fine."

But she reached for him, pushed him into a chair with surprising strength.

Even worse, he went. Big, bad, tough Sam O'Brien fell into a chair simply because she'd urged him to.

Then her fingers touched the bare skin on his neck, and as if he'd been poked by a hot stick, he surged to his feet.

At his quick movement, a sweet laugh escaped

her and she clasped her hands in front of her. "I'm sorry, I'm just so nervous about being here. I have to answer some more questions, and it's…" She looked away. Swallowed hard. "It's, um, giving me a bit of a bad time."

Ah, hell. "No one is going to push you," he heard himself say. "They'll go slow and easy."

"I know." She backed to the door. "Anyway, I'm sorry. Again." She was sorry because she'd touched him and he nearly bolted right out of the chair as if he'd been goosed.

She'd turned him on, this woman of the bright yellow sundress, silly blue glasses, sweet smile and expressive eyes. And the shocking jolt of arousal—*arousal,* for God's sake—had nearly caused his heart to leap out of his chest.

He was at work, damn it, and if there was one thing he disliked, it was when something distracted him from his work. "I have to get back to my job," he said, his voice more than a bit strained.

"Oh! Of course." But her gaze caught at something on his desk and she went wide-eyed.

"What is it?"

Hands over her mouth, she stared at a composite drawing he'd gotten just that morning, of someone he suspected to be deep in the thick of the identity-theft ring he was trying to crack.

She looked pale. Why had he let her in his office? Why hadn't he showed her the door two minutes ago? "What's the matter?" he asked again, hoping she wasn't really going to tell him, hoping she'd simply take her perky little self and go away. Far away. And take the flowers with her.

"Is he…wanted?"

"Yes. Why?"

"Well, because I've seen him downtown."

This particular suspect had laid low all year, hiding out from the best of the best on the force, including himself. They didn't even know his name, had only his description from his latest victim, whom he'd conned out of his ID with a door-to-door sales scam. Much as he'd like to have her solve his problem by locating the suspect, he'd followed too many dead ends to believe her.

Angie picked up the picture and studied it carefully, and he studied her just as carefully.

Her fingernails matched her toenails, he noted, but were chipped and nibbled at. Probably her line of work, he figured, then rolled his eyes at himself.

He was noticing her *nails,* for God's sake.

Man, he needed a break. A vacation. Yeah, that was it. Maybe Hawaii, with a few bikini-clad babes.

Too bad he never took vacations.

"I do know him," she said.

"From?"

"I can't remember exactly."

He took the picture from her hands. "If you think of it, call in."

Those expressive eyes stared at him. "You don't believe me."

Maybe that was because she thought his walls should be pink. Or that she had dreamed of being a cop when she was afraid of weapons. But telling her so felt a little like kicking a puppy. "It's nothing personal. We get hundreds of false leads."

She crossed her arms and held her ground, reminding him that while she could look so vulnerable, she was actually tough as hell. "You think I'm a silly little flake."

There was no mistaking her hurt now, and he swore at himself. "No—"

"But you don't think I've seen this guy."

"Okay, fine." He leaned back against his desk, the desk now covered in flowers. He was going to smell like a garden. "Where do you know him from? What's his name? What does he do?"

"I don't know." She took a step back, making him feel like the school-yard bully. "I just know that I've seen him coming and going in the used bookstore next to the café where I work."

He studied her a long moment, considering. She seemed genuine enough. "You're certain."

"Absolutely."

"Those glasses don't look too reliable."

"I can see perfectly."

He sighed. "Fine. I'll check it out."

The look she shot him was purely female, purely annoyed. "But you don't expect to find him, right?"

"Well…"

"Truthfully."

How to tell her how many false leads he'd followed? How many times people thought they saw one thing but in reality saw another? "Look—"

"Oh, never mind." She sent him a smile, completely devoid of the brilliance from before, which for some reason made Sam hurt inside.

"Angie—"

"No, really." She lifted a hand to ward him off. "You're busy. Don't give it another thought." She headed to the door. "I'm going to go answer those questions now."

"Yeah. Angie—"

"Bye, Sam."

Then she was gone and he was staring at the

door, torn between relief and a self-disgust because he knew he'd been curt and rude.

Damn, he hated working with people.

Chapter 3

Angie got up at the crack of dawn, as always. She drove to work, as always. She figured she'd enter the café fifteen minutes before her shift, then help Elisa prepare for the breakfast shift. As always.

But nothing was as always at all, because with one twist of fate—and a very sharp knife—she could have died, and unexpectedly she was still dealing with the horror of that.

And then there was Detective Sam O'Brien. He'd both saved her life and changed it forever, because she'd taken a look into those deep, fathomless, brooding eyes and had seen her future. It sounded silly now, in the sharp, glaring light of a new day, and at the memory of how he'd treated her in his office, she blushed.

If *that* was her future, feeling like a ball of un-important fluff, she didn't want it, thank you very much. Been there, bought the T-shirt.

Yes, he'd been sweet and kind during her bank ordeal, and yes, darn it, maybe as a result she'd looked at him with stars in her eyes, but now those stars were *so* long gone.

She was better off by herself.

But she *was* going to find his suspect. Oh yes, that would be satisfying, if nothing else, just to prove she wasn't the kind of person who made these things up to get attention.

She didn't need attention, not from him. What she needed was to stick to her guns and live her life. She liked the feeling that coursed through her at that thought. This new-lease-on-life-thing felt good. Empowering.

Yeah. And next time she got held up, she wouldn't need a hero, she'd save herself.

As if her karma was in perfect sync, on the walk to work she caught a glimpse of a man striding away from her, down the alley between the café and the used bookstore.

She knew that short, dark crew cut. She knew those tennis shoes, that compact, muscle-bound body, as she'd seen him several times now, either loitering in front of the bookstore where she spent far too many hours and too much of her tips, or as he was now, walking down the alley.

He was also the man she'd seen in the picture on Sam's desk.

He was Sam's suspect, and visions of proving him wrong and her right danced in her head. So did visions of getting herself killed, but she was too fond of her new life at the moment to let that happen.

Besides, contrary to popular belief by one stubborn detective, she had a brain. She knew better than to try to stop a wanted man by herself.

To prove it, she fumbled in her purse for the cell phone she'd won just last month in a mailer sweepstakes. At the time she'd thought she'd much rather have won a year's supply of groceries, but right now she was grateful for the phone.

And the fact that for once her battery was fully charged.

Dialing 911, heart pounding, Angie flattened herself against the wall of the building, holding her breath when the man paused and glanced over his shoulder.

From nearly fifty feet, their gazes met and locked.

"Emergency dispatch," came a female voice in her ear.

"I need to talk to Sam O'Brien," Angie whispered, swallowing hard as fear turned her stomach to mush. "He's a detective with—"

"Ma'am, you need to dial him direct—this is not an answering service."

"It's an emergency." This whole calling-a-cop thing looked so much easier on television. "I have one of his suspects in sight right this very minute, and I think he'd want to know."

"Where are you and what's your name?"

Sam's suspect stared at her for exactly two more seconds before vanishing around a corner.

Angie grated her teeth and gave the dispatcher the information, knowing it would be too late. "Tell Sam to hurry, and that if he needs me I'll be working in the café." Frustrated, she stood there staring down the alley, wishing she was a police officer so she could go find the guy herself.

The war between doing just that and staying put wasn't a hard one to fight. She knew better. And anyway, despite feeling strong and sure, she didn't have quite enough nerve.

But she'd give anything to be a big, tough, armed cop at this moment. With one last sigh, she entered the café.

"About time," her boss groused as she came into the kitchen.

Angie hung up her sweater, pulled a hair band out of her pocket and tied up her hair. "Good morning to you, too. And I'm not late. I'm early."

"Hmph." Josephine looked at her and let out a huff. "It should be illegal to look as good as you do wearing that ugly uniform and your hair all piled on top of your head like that." She continued slicing cantaloupe as she sighed, and on her two-hundred-plus-pound frame, the sound was substantial. "Why aren't you in bed after your ordeal?"

"My *ordeal* was two days ago. Besides, I'd be bored to tears in bed."

"Not if you put a man in there first."

"Yeah, well…" Angie reached for her apron. A man in her bed had never brought her anything but a vague sense that she was missing something. "You should know, there might be some excitement here in a few minutes."

"Excitement?"

The heavy knock at the back door caused Angie to jump. Casually as she could, she opened the door and faced one glowering Sam O'Brien.

He was imposing, intense, and very unsmiling.

"You got my message," she said, amazed and trying not to gape at the oddly thrilling sight of his big, tough body standing there. "I didn't think the dispatcher would tell you. She thought I was a prank call."

"Was it?"

"Was it what?"

"A prank call," he said slowly, through his teeth, towering over her.

"Of course not." She had to remind herself that just because he was breathtaking didn't mean he couldn't be a complete jerk. Although that seemed a bit unfair, because she could remember quite vividly how gently and warmly he'd held her, talking her through the aftermath of the holdup.

Where had that man gone?

"Did you look down the alley?" she asked.

"Yes. And in the still-closed bookstore. And in all the neighboring alleys. There's no one out there, Angie. No one."

"He was."

He closed his eyes and shoved a hand through his hair. Then he leveled her with a look that made her want to cringe. It was *that* look, the one that said she didn't know what she was talking about, and if she did, it probably wasn't important anyway.

She was very tired of that look, of feeling invisible. It came from being average, she thought, annoyed with herself. All her life she'd been so average most people had never even noticed her.

And she'd allowed it.

That would have to change, too. Maybe she'd go blond. No, that would only multiply the ditzy image. Redhead? Hmm, something to think about. "I saw him," she repeated, raising her chin, refusing to let him make her feel stupid again. "And if you lost him, it's your own fault. You need to respond faster."

"I got here in less than five minutes from your original call," he pointed out, still through his teeth, his huge body practically quivering with temper.

What was it about her that brought out the worst in people? Another thing she intended to change. Thinking only to soothe, she reached out and put her hand on his arm.

The considerable amount of muscles beneath his skin jerked, but he controlled himself with nothing more than pure willpower.

She understood the effort, if not the reasoning. She too felt an almost physical jolt. Unnerved, she dropped her hand.

He stared at her for a long moment before pulling a business card from his pocket. "Take this. It's got my office and cell numbers on it. Call me direct next time."

The air whooshed out of her lungs. "You believe me?"

He put his sunglasses on. "I don't know."

"You believe me." She grinned, ridiculously relieved, even when his frown returned.

"But if you're in danger, call 911. Got that?"

"Yes. So which number should I call next time I see him?"

Sam looked pained. "You won't."

"I think I will."

"Angie—"

"I'm not making this up, Sam. He's out there. I'll see him again."

"No one else has."

"Because no one else is out there at this time of morning. I think he's an early bird."

He sighed again, as if she was making his life a living hell on purpose. "You realize this guy is considered dangerous, right? Don't—"

"Don't do anything stupid?" She tried not to care that he thought she would. "I won't."

"If you think you see him again—"

"Not think. *Know.*"

"If you think you see him again," he repeated firmly, "stay safe. Stay far away. *Really* far away. Then call me."

"Call you."

"Yeah. Me." He didn't look thrilled. "But if you're in any sort of danger at all, I mean it, Angie, if he so much as blinks at you, call 911. Immediately."

"Like I did this time."

His eyes narrowed. "Are you telling me he saw you?"

"And listened to me call for help."

He swore, winced, then again shoved his fingers through his hair. "Terrific. Look—" His radio crackled, and someone called to him, requesting him as backup. "Damn. We'll finish this later."

She wondered if that was a threat or a promise, and decided by the look on his face it was a chore. "No need. I'll contact you when I see him again."

When the door had shut behind him, Angie turned to see Josephine brimming with curiosity.

"Was that your cop?"

"Not *my* cop. *The* cop."

"Uh-huh." Josephine looked bowled over. "He was…wow."

"Oh, close your mouth, you're going to catch flies."

"I guess we're not going to talk about how *wow* he was."

"Did I mention I registered for college?"

"Nice subject change."

"Yep."

Josephine put her hands on her ample hips. "Honey, listen. I don't mean to interfere—"

"Yes, you do."

"Hush. I'm talking, and what I'm talking about is you getting over what's-his-name and finding another man. Like Mr. Wow Cop for example."

"I'm over what's-his-name." Definitely over Tony. *So* over Tony—ex-fiancé, ex-friend, ex-everything. Maybe still recovering, still getting her balance, but not mourning.

Life was too darn short.

"Lordie, that man was *hot*." Josephine fanned herself. "And I bet he wouldn't let you out of bed so early."

Angie laughed, but a small part of her tingled at the thought of finding a man who wouldn't let her out of bed because he couldn't stand to be without her.

She hadn't a clue what that would be like.

"Angie, honey, you know I love you."

Angie smiled. "Does this mean I'm getting a raise?"

"Uh…no. But I worry. You shouldn't be here today just because I don't have anyone to cover the shift. You should take some time off."

"I'm fine."

"Fine is good, and good is crap. But never mind that now. The point is you deserve more."

"Like I said, I'm going to college. Oh, and I bought myself a book just the other day."

"A romance?"

"Well, no."

Josephine snorted in disgust.

"But it was good," Angie insisted. "And I've got lots of changes in the works. Big ones."

"Really? You're going to read a romance?"

"Much bigger."

"Uh-huh. How about we just pretend to see that suspect so your cop will come back. Just once, pretty please?"

Luke stood in an interrogation room in front of their witness, Lou, who was seated in a chair.

Sam stood behind him.

Lou fidgeted nervously. He had a stack of petty crimes against him, all of which Sam could make go away.

For an exchange, that is. A good one. Such as one damn lead on their case.

Luke slowly paced the room. "So." He stopped in front of Lou and smiled, his eyes warm and encouraging. "You have an uncle who has a neighbor, who has a girlfriend, who's friends with the guy who offered you a new identity for three hundred. Right?"

"Yeah." Lou licked his lips, warming up to Luke. "That's all. I didn't ask for it or nothing, you know? They just thought…" He bit his fingernail.

"That you'd like to skip out on your crimes." This from Sam, whose voice was hard as steel. He stayed behind Lou, wishing he could wring his scrawny, stupid little neck.

"No. *No,*" Lou said, forced to twist around in his chair to eyeball Sam, who did not smile warmly and encouragingly. "I don't need a new identity." Sweat broke out on his brow. "I'm innocent. Totally innocent."

"Yeah. As a shark."

"Now, Sam." Luke shot him a "be patient" look. "Let's give Lou a break."

They were playing good-cop bad-cop. Not a stretch for Sam to be the tough one. "I'll give him a break when he gives me one. I want the—"

"The bigger fish?" Lou broke in hopefully.

"That's right," Luke soothed. "The bigger fish. The *other* guys. You can help us, Lou. It'd be good for you to help us."

"You want to take down the entire identity-theft ring."

"With your help," Luke said.

Lou started to sweat more. "But I told you already, man. I know nothing. Nothing at all."

"You know enough, I think," Luke said pleasantly.

"No, Luke, maybe Lou here is right." Sam came around front and stared at Lou coldly. "Maybe he can't help us. Never you mind, Lou. We'll just take you down the hall, book you, and—"

"What?" Lou cried, shrinking back, shoving his hands into his pockets as if to avoid the cuffs. "But you just said you don't care what I've done."

"Not if you help us." Luke smiled again. Sweet as an innocent babe. "Why don't you help us, Lou?"

"Don't bother, he doesn't want to." Sam pulled out a pair of handcuffs, yelled for a guard and walked toward Lou.

"Okay, okay!" Lou shot them a shaky smile as sweat poured down his face. "Sheesh. Maybe I can get you…something."

"Now you're talking," Luke said very kindly. "Keep going."

"Uh…"

Sam held up the cuffs and raised an eyebrow. Waiting.

Lou sighed. "Okay, listen. The kid making the new IDs…he's some computer whiz kid at P.C.C."

"If he's a whiz kid, why is he going to Pasadena

City College instead of a four-year school?" Luke asked.

"No money."

Sam thought about this then shook his head. "Don't buy it. This guy, if he's the right one, is making a fortune off this gig. Two hundred thousand last month alone."

"He's not the boss, he's just a paid joker."

"Who is the boss?"

"Don't know."

"Give us a name," Luke coaxed. "That'll be a good start."

"John."

Sam rolled his eyes. "That's convenient. How about a last name, ace?"

"That's all I know," Lou insisted. "That's all I know."

When they were back in Sam's office, Luke looked at Sam very seriously. "I've got to ask."

"Okay," Sam said, expecting a question on the case.

"Get any more flowers today, lover boy?"

Luke was grinning at him, the bastard. "You know I didn't."

"Then you didn't play your cards right."

"Luke?"

"Yeah?"

"Shut up."

Luke merely laughed. "You're still in the papers this morning, did you see that? Such a hero, our Sam. Can I have your autograph?"

Each of them had been through some pretty rough times, and each of them had come through with different attitudes. Luke tended to put his emotions out there, despite his toughness.

Sam did not.

Sam didn't like to acknowledge his emotions in any way, shape or form. They had disappointed and hurt him once too often.

Anyway, for all those reasons, or maybe none of them, Luke's dark eyes rarely did that sparkle dance thing as they were doing now, no matter how amused he might be.

Nice as that was to see, Sam didn't care for it being at his own expense, even if he was aware Luke was just trying to get a rise out of him.

If only Luke knew, just thinking about Angie got a rise out of him. "Can we talk the case, do you think, or do you want to joke around all day?"

"Sorry."

"You don't look sorry. You look disgustingly…I don't know. Happy."

Luke lifted a shoulder. "Maybe I got lucky last night."

"With Sara?"

"Maybe."

"About time. You've been dating her a month."

"Some things are worth waiting for."

Sam eyeballed the known womanizer Luke Sorrintino. "That sounds serious."

Luke shrugged again and turned away.

"Oh, now that we're talking about you, we're done?"

"That's right. Besides, our little problem awaits us— Well, *hello*." Luke smiled broadly at someone in the doorway, and even before Sam glanced over and saw his partner's flirtatious expression, he knew.

Angie.

She stood there with her sweet face smiling right at him, in her secondhand glasses that emphasized her huge eyes and a floral, gauzy dress covered in sunflowers that made him wish he had a pair of sunglasses just to look at her.

"You look tense again," she said to Sam. "Am I interrupting?"

Yes.

"Of course not," Luke said before Sam could speak. "We were just questioning a witness. I was the good cop. Sam here…" They both turned to stare at him.

"I bet he makes a scary bad cop," Angie said with a secret little smile.

As if she knew him.

Well, if she did, and she could read his mind right now, she'd know this terrible urge he had to go to her, *touch* her. She'd probably run screaming from the room.

"You catch far more flies with honey instead of vinegar," she said, wrinkling her nose delicately as she looked around his office with a sort of morbid curiosity.

"A mess, isn't it?" Luke tsked, and Sam glared at him.

"I suggested opening the shades and fumigating," Angie said. "But he wasn't interested."

"No, he's very tense, our Sam."

Oh, very funny.

"At the very least, he should try aromatherapy," Angie said told Luke.

"I agree. I mean, just look at him." Now Luke sidled over toward Angie, so that both of them were looking back at him; his partner with laughter in his eyes, and Angie, with…uh-oh. An unmistakable spurt of…something, all right. Something that made his insides do a juvenile sort of quiver. Damn it, he thought he'd taken care of that the last time they'd stood in this office together.

No attraction between them. Not now, not ever.

He faced them both. "I don't need sunshine, fumigating or aromatherapy, thank you." He took Luke's arm, showed him the door and closed it behind him.

"Before you say a word," Angie said. "I just wanted to say, I didn't come here to discuss the horrid color of your walls or the way you keep your office."

"But you had to mention it."

"Well, yes. Since I was here." She smiled, a totally disarming smile. "That was just a bonus suggestion, you understand, and I'll try to restrain myself in the future. I'm not here to make a pest of myself."

Oddly enough, she wasn't. Because somehow, simply by standing there, his day seemed... brighter.

Not good. "I'm pretty busy."

Her smile dimmed slightly, and he wondered what exactly it was about her that made him such a jerk. "I wanted to see that picture again," she said.

"Picture?" All he could think of was the photo of them in the paper, when she'd been snuggled against his chest, when he'd been staring down into her face—

"The suspect drawing."

"Oh." *Idiot.* "It's here…somewhere." He went to his desk and started rifling, nearly growling when she came close and leaned over his desk, too, her sweet-smelling hair brushing his arm.

"Sorry," she said, tossing it over her shoulder. "I tend to get in people's spaces. I know you don't like to be touched."

Oh, he liked to be touched. Sexually, that is. Which, unfortunately, was suddenly all he could think about at the moment. "Here." He found the picture before he made a fool of himself and pulled it from the disaster masquerading as his desk. "What did you need it for?"

"I just wanted to add…" She took the paper, set it on the desk, reached for a pencil and—

"Hey, that's—"

"Yes," she breathed, straightening, holding up the sheet to inspect her handiwork. "That's it. Now it's perfect."

Sam grabbed the composite drawing and stared at it. She'd added a little goatee.

"Something about the rendering has been bothering me." She peeked over his shoulder, which she had to stand on tiptoe to do. He could imagine her a little closer, just enough that her breasts would press into his back and—

"I couldn't place it right away," she said softly, clearly having no idea his thoughts had taken him to the gutter. "Not until I saw him again."

Sam stepped clear and faced her, not allowing himself to look anywhere but into her dark eyes. "You…saw him again?"

"Not since I called you, no. I'll let you know if anything else comes to me. Well, I know you're too busy to stand around talking, so…"

Sam stared at her, but all he saw was her pretty little behind as it sashayed toward his door. "Where are you going?"

"To work," she said. "I skipped the bank this morning. Still don't feel comfortable going inside. I'm finally replacing my lost ATM card."

She made his head spin. "Angie—"

But she was gone.

Two days later, Sam and Luke were still checking on every "John" registered at P.C.C. when Sam's cell phone rang.

"Sorry to bother you," Angie said in his ear. "But Mr. Suspect just walked down the alley between the café and the bookstore. And you know, I keep forgetting to ask you. What's his name? What's he wanted for?"

"We don't know his name and he's part of an identity-theft ring—wait." He shook his head to clear the strange pleasure that had come over him at hearing her musical voice. No matter how much he ignored her, she'd been in the back of his mind. Hell, okay, the *front* of his mind. "You saw him?"

"That's why I'm calling, Sam."

Lord, she was going to give him gray hair before he hit thirty-five. "Angie."

"Yes?"

"Stay right where you are." He pulled a U-turn to head back across town. "Don't even think about going after him yourself."

She didn't say anything, and a bad, bad feeling overcame the good one he'd had at the sound of her. "I mean it, Angie. If you—"

"I hear you perfectly well, Sam," she said in a rather subdued voice. "And believe it or not, I even understand the English language, so there's no need to repeat yourself. I won't go after him myself, that would be stupid."

When the dial tone sounded in his ear, he swore and tossed the phone aside.

"Angie?" Luke asked.

"Yeah."

"Trouble?"

"Yeah." Sam sped them toward the café and tried not to panic over all the possible scenarios Angie was creating at that very moment. "Big trouble."

"Isn't that just like a woman."

Chapter 4

Twenty minutes later, Sam had searched the alley, the closed bookstore, the café, the parking lot in back…everywhere. He'd showed pictures of their suspect to the few people he found on the street, but no one, not a single soul, had seen him.

Other than Angie.

Luke came back from the alley, which he'd walked yet again, shaking his head. "No sign of life back there anywhere."

Sam sighed, rubbed his aching temples and turned toward Angie. She stood in the opened doorway of the café, apron on, hair haphazardly piled on top of her head. Half in shadow, half in sunlight, her body was clearly outlined. Legs, nice and toned. Softly curved hips. Perfectly rounded breasts straining the front of her blouse. And for a moment, his brain assimilated her not as a victim, not a responsibility, but as a woman. All woman.

A woman who was looking at him hopefully.

Slowly he shook his head.

She turned away, as if she was disappointed in *him,* of all things. As if it was *his* fault she was crazy.

"Angie."

"I have customers," she said over her shoulder. "Sorry to have bothered you again." And then she shut the door.

"Like I said," Luke offered. "Just like a woman."

Luke waited until they were nearly back at the station to speculate. "She's awfully sweet. Sort of whimsical, I think. And strong as hell, given what she went through at the bank."

Sam would have said tenacious. Stubborn. "How about pain in the ass."

Luke arched a brow.

"And annoying," Sam added, getting into it. Damn, why had she given him that look of disappointment? Was he doomed to get that look from every single female in his life? Not that she was in his life. Nope. No way. "And really irritating."

"Annoying and irritating are the same thing," Luke pointed out. "Anything else?"

"Yeah. She drives me crazy."

"You're being kind of tough on her, aren't you?"

She'd only barged into his life unannounced, unexpected and unwanted. And had stayed there. "I'm tough on everyone."

"Yes." Luke nodded thoughtfully. "And most can't hack it."

Which was why Sam had never remarried after his one short, disastrous union with Kim. It was why his own mother was so disappointed in him. "So?"

"So," Luke said in a patient voice that made Sam want to slug him. "I don't think Angie fits into the 'most' category."

"What are you saying?"

"That you're not going to scare her off with the bad-cop thing. That despite the fact she's young, and maybe even a touch naive, she looks pretty tough to me. Not only that, she's…"

"What?"

Luke smiled. "Hot. Very hot."

"Luke?"

Luke turned toward him. "Let me guess. Shut up?"

"Please."

College started. Angie had decided on several general education classes after talking to a college advisor who'd suggested a teaching career.

Teaching art…it appealed in a way she hadn't imagined. She could use her passion and still make a living. On her first night of class, she nearly burst with pride as she picked a seat among the students and soaked up the next hour.

She loved it. Loved everything about it: the smell of the room, the desk that made her bottom numb, the thirst for knowledge all around her.

Okay, it was only *her* thirst. All the other students were younger, more hip…and bored.

Which made no sense to her at all. Nothing about it bored her, not when she was finally there. Which probably explained why she'd grinned like an idiot all the way through the English lecture that put just about every other student in the room to sleep.

The self-pride sustained her all the way home, in her 1974 VW Bug that had seen better days. It wasn't the lack of money in her checkbook that kept her loyal to the ancient clunker, though that was why she hadn't gotten the pale blue Bug the paint job it long ago deserved.

She simply loved the car. It'd been her first, bought with hard-earned money she'd saved from her various assortment of jobs over the years, and she saw no reason to change it.

Her entire life was changing. In light of that, keeping the old Bug was a sort of security blanket. Her one allowed weakness from the past.

She could live with that.

Her phone was ringing when she pulled into the carport next to her apartment. The place had been built in the early 1920s, and was a bit run-down since its last renovation in the early 70s, but she loved it, too. The wraparound porch, the myriad little windows and turrets…the place had charm and personality and never failed to warm her heart when she came home.

Though it sat on prime land in South Pasadena, and by rights should have been far out of her rent bracket, she got the place for practically nothing. Mostly because she kept up the yard, and also because she always had time to chat with Mrs. Penrow, who'd owned the place for more than fifty years.

As Angie hustled through the small, cozy and

comfortably overgrown yard, with the grass she needed to cut this weekend, and the daisies just beginning to take over the ground at the rosebushes' roots, her phone continued to ring.

The hour was late, which meant, darn it, it wouldn't be Ed McMahon saying she'd won the Publisher's Clearing House Sweepstakes.

"What are you doing up this late?" her mother demanded when Angie finally answered just as her machine picked up.

Given the heavy breathing accompanying her mother's voice, her father was on the extension as well. "How do you know I'm still up?" Angie asked, her good mood holding. For the moment. "Maybe you woke me."

"Oh!" Her mother sounded horrified and apologetic. "Did I?"

"No." Angie smiled because she was still so thrilled with how her night had gone. She should have done this long ago, so very long ago. Why hadn't she? Why had it taken a near tragedy? Didn't matter, she decided. And though she knew her parents would misunderstand, she had to tell them. "Mom. Dad." She took a deep breath. "I took my first college course tonight."

"Oh my God!" Her mother squealed with shock

and delight. "You're going to be a doctor after all! My daughter, the doctor."

"No, Mom—"

"This is wonderful! Why didn't you tell us you'd enrolled in medical school?"

Some of Angie's glow started to recede. "Mom, you have to get a bachelor's degree before you can go to medical school."

"So you'll get a bachelor's degree. How long will it take?"

"But I never wanted to be a doctor. I want—"

"Sure you did. When you were a little girl, you used to love to carry that little toy medical kit around and fix up all your stuffed animals."

A headache started between Angie's eyes as her newfound determination warred with her age-old need to please them.

"And then all through high school we talked about you getting scholarships—"

"I never had the grades for that, Mom. And we both know, being a doctor was never for me. It was for you."

Utter silence. Even her father didn't have a comment. At first.

"I'm sorry to speak so bluntly," she said. "You've never wanted to hear this. You probably don't want to hear it now, but…well, things have changed for me."

"Because of the holdup." Her mother's voice softened. "You're still in shock, you—"

"I'm not in shock. But I did get a wake-up call. I mean I could have d—"

"Don't say it," her mother interrupted fiercely.

"But it's the truth. I could have died, without ever really having lived my life. I don't want that to happen, Mom. Can't you try to understand that? I want to go after something from my own heart."

"I thought Tony was your heart. What a wonderful man. And a lawyer! You could try to get him back."

They knew nothing of what had split the two of them up, and yet they assumed Tony had left her. Not a surprise, Angie supposed, but just once she would have liked the benefit of the doubt.

Tony had been a prime example of bad judgment. A serious lapse. He was everything her parents had ever wanted in a son-in-law. Educated, smart, independently wealthy.

And he'd never ever really known Angie, or even tried to. The pressure had been similar to what her parents had put on her to be someone she wasn't, and she'd nearly suffocated. To combat it, she'd done nothing with herself. She'd stagnated. "Tony wasn't the one for me."

"You say that because he left. But how could a perfect man not be the one?"

"Tony and I wouldn't have made a happy couple. Being a doctor wouldn't have made me happy either. But," she said quickly before she could get interrupted again, "college does."

"Oh." Her mother sighed. "Well, it's a nice start. Frank, maybe you can talk to her about a medical degree—"

"No. Look, I'm nearly twenty-six years old." Angie talked as she flipped through her mail. "I'm going to do this my way, okay?" She realized that the "okay" part of the sentence left room for debate. "I'll let you know how it goes," she said more firmly.

Then she saw the package that had come for her, and she smiled again. "I have to go. Got the early shift in the morning."

"After college, you'll be able to get a real job."

Her mother never gave up. "I gotta go. Love you, bye." Then she hung up quickly so she couldn't hear any more disappointment or doubt. She didn't need that right now, the extra tug on her emotions that might cause her to give up.

No more giving up. Ever.

With that in mind, she tore into the package she'd been waiting for. She'd ordered it after the holdup, when she'd realized her life had nearly been extinguished before she'd ever even lived it, when she'd realized there was more out there for her than waking up and going to sleep.

When she'd realized Sam made her heart quiver.

Of course that was also before she'd realized he was not so different from the others in her world. Condescending. Unaccepting.

But she was human. And as a very human female, she did know, no matter what he thought, that she could help him with his case. She *had* seen his witness and she knew she'd see him again.

Pulling the fingerprinting kit free of its wrapping, she reached for the directions and began to read.

It was three days before Angie saw the suspect again. Three days in which she was aware of every hour, every moment. She absorbed another class. She took a long walk every morning and concentrated on the beauty around her. She read voraciously.

She lived. And as a result, she felt unbelievably... alive.

Yet she still avoided the bank. Strong as she told

herself she was, she wasn't quite that strong. But by the end of the coming week, she knew she'd have to get over that particular fear, as she'd simply have to get money into her account.

A worry for Friday, she told herself. Besides, maybe her newly ordered ATM card would come.

She went to work thinking that this very moment was the first day of the rest of her life. From now on, every day was the first day of the rest of her life.

It felt good. It put a little bounce in her step as she went up the steps to the café. Reaching for the door, she glanced over her shoulder and noticed a car pulling into the alley.

Many cars went down the alley every day: for deliveries, for workers going in and out the back of their buildings, for people looking for a shortcut through traffic, so why she noticed this nondescript color and model, she didn't know.

But things were different these days. She paid attention to everything. She'd even put on mascara and lip gloss this morning. The woman in the reflection of her mirror had looked…happy.

Oh, yes, she was proud of herself, and liked it. She hadn't even had a single nightmare last night, not about bank drawers or knives or threats…not a one.

Then something warm slithered around her calf and she leaped into the air.

"Meow."

"Saber." Josephine's cat. Angie let out a gasping laugh and put a hand to her racing heart before she hunkered down to pet the twenty-two-pound tabby. The cat sprawled shamelessly on her back, a loud purr rumbling. "No scraps yet this morning," Angie said, amused. "Though by the looks of you, you don't need any." She came to her feet.

Now there were two men standing by the car in the alley. The first man, dressed casually in jeans and a T-shirt, moved out of sight, but before he did, Angie jerked with recognition.

Sam's suspect.

The other, a tall and elegantly dressed man, didn't walk away. He was on a cell phone.

"I'll be there in half an hour. I've just got a quick errand," Angie overheard him say. Then he pocketed the phone and walked in the opposite direction without a backward glance.

Angie stood there, staring at the car, feeling the weight of her fingerprinting kit in her purse. Her cell phone was there, too.

Options raced through her head. Call Sam, of course. Which would, no doubt, end in her humiliating herself once more.

She could call the police anonymously. Leave a tip. She'd seen enough American's Most Wanted to know they wanted any and all leads, even if she turned out to be wrong. No one there would look at her as if she needed to have her head examined.

Last option—she could do nothing.

But that wasn't in her nature. At least not anymore. With a sigh, she thought of Sam again. She could already see his frustration. But this wasn't about Sam. No, it was about her. And proving herself.

Being held up in that bank, being saved by him… it had all definitely been one of the most terrifying yet oddly thrilling experiences of her life, which really, when she thought about it, was a sad statement on her existence to date.

But no more. She had strength and courage and a great future.

Calling Sam was the right thing to do, no matter that he would give her the look that told her he was torn between irritation and honor, between wanting to wring her neck for bothering him, and needing to make sure she really was a loon before ignoring her.

The woman who cried wolf. That's who he thought she was. A thrill seeker. A hanger-on.

She was none of those things, and she wanted him to know it. She'd take his suspect's prints with her new kit, and *then* she'd call him. She'd give him the prints. She'd take charge.

Yep, first day of the rest of her life. She moved toward the car. Not being completely stupid, she glanced up and down the alley first, but there was no one in sight. Surely she had enough time to get a print, then get out of the way and make the call.

She set her tools down on the ground, knelt by the door handle and concentrated on the directions she'd memorized. It wasn't as easy under pressure, and she messed up her first try. But before she could try again, she heard a noise and rushed to her feet. As she did, she reached into her pocket for her cell phone, and—

Came face-to-face with a police officer who didn't look nearly as happy to see her as she was to see him.

"What are you doing?" he asked.

"Oh, Officer, great." She sent him a megawatt smile, both because he'd scared the living daylights out of her, and because she was relieved it was a cop who had managed to sneak up on her, not a bad guy. "I was just going to call you."

"Really. What a coincidence."

"Yes. I have reason to believe that the owner of this car is a wanted man."

"Wanted for what?"

"What's going on here?" A man stepped out. Not the suspect, but the tall, elegantly dressed one, and he looked more than a touch annoyed. "This is my car."

The officer looked at Angie.

Angie sighed. "I thought the other guy owned the car, the one who came with this man."

The man shook his head. "I'm alone."

"But I saw him. He was standing right next to you in the alley."

"There was never anyone with me this morning."

It was the officer's turn to sigh. "It's too early for this."

"I'll say." The owner brushed past her, inspected the door for scratches, then gestured for Angie to move out of his way so he could get in.

"You're going to let him go?" Angie asked the officer.

"I'm going to let *you* go."

"Yeah." She supposed she'd have to start the rest of her life tomorrow.

She went to see Sam in his lion's den—er, his office. She refrained from making any cracks about the condition of his office, but it wasn't easy.

And given the vaguely amused way he watched her as she entered, he knew it.

"You should know," she said right off, wanting to just spit it out. "I had a little chat with a very nice policeman today in the alley where I was attempting to take fingerprints off a car I thought was your suspect's."

He blinked, shook his head, blinked again and still didn't appear to be able to speak.

"I know you're going to say I shouldn't have interfered, but it's done. And no, I didn't get the prints. Turns out I'm not quite as adept as I thought I was."

He rose out of his chair and came to stand in front of her. He slowly reached out, cupped her jaw and stared into her face. "First of all, are you hurt?"

His fingers on her skin sent an electrical charge through her body, not that she could concentrate on that through her confusion. She'd been so certain he'd be furious. Why wasn't he furious? "Um…no. I'm not hurt. Not at all."

"Well, thank God for small favors. Now tell me what happened."

"I saw two men by the car. One was your suspect. I had looked down for just a minute but assumed he'd gotten out of the same car and—"

"And he didn't, I take it."

"No. And then the other guy thought I was some sort of a loon, so the policeman wasn't happy with me. I realized after I left that I didn't even get the car's license plate number." She bit her lower lip, waited for his annoyance. His frustration.

Instead, his thumb continued to stroke her jaw, his gaze following the motion intensely.

She almost wished he wouldn't, because she was looking at him, feeling him, seeing an almost… tender side she hadn't realized existed.

She was a sucker for tender. "Sam?"

With a sigh, his eyes cleared. He dropped his hand. "You terrify me, you know that?"

"Why?"

"What if the other guy had come back and found you alone in the alley?"

"Well, I thought they were together, you see, and the first man, the owner of the car, was talking into his cell phone and he said he'd be a half an hour, so I thought…"

"You thought you were safe," he finished grimly, and shoved his fingers through his hair. "Promise me you won't do anything like that again."

She looked into his eyes, saw his intensity, his worry for her. She really wanted to be able to make the promise, she really did. She wanted a whole heck of a lot, she was discovering, when it came to him. "Sam, I can help you on this case."

He closed his eyes and sighed again. And when he opened them back up, she saw another heart-stopping flash of that tenderness.

"Angie, I know you felt helpless at the bank holdup. I know you felt weak and defenseless, when you're none of those things. But making up for it by catching a different bad guy isn't the answer. I want you to promise me you won't do anything like this again."

"I can promise you I won't get hurt," she said softly, begging him with her eyes to understand. To let her help.

But he shook his head and turned away, staring blindly out the window. "That's a promise you can't keep, so let's not even go there."

The end of the week came. The entire seven days had been one big exercise in frustration for Sam. The holdup. Angie. The consequential newspaper extravaganza. Angie. The calls. The paperwork.

Angie.

She just wouldn't go away, and yet she confused the hell out of him because even as she wanted to be in his life to solve his case—which still bugged him—she didn't want to be *in* his life.

And yet in his experience, women wanted in. So what made Angie so different? Why couldn't he put her out of his mind?

Because he was afraid she was going to get herself killed, that's why. It was that simple. He had the incident in the alley as an example.

No doubt, she terrified him.

He just had no idea what to do about it. So he checked on her. Stopped by the café. Stopped by her apartment.

All in the name of duty.

Mostly.

Angie turned out to be a busy woman, not as easy to peg as he'd imagined. Which is how he found himself three mornings in a row sitting in the kitchen of the café, drinking the best coffee he'd ever had, bantering with Josephine and watching Angie when she wasn't looking.

No doubt, she loved what she did. She made that clear with every smile, every laugh, every touch. She remembered orders without writing them down, and always had a kind word. It was amazing.

She was amazing.

She was also the sweetest, most giving, warmest woman he'd ever met. And completely guileless. If he'd harbored any doubt of her sincerity and naiveté, it'd vanished while watching her serve her customers those mornings.

God help him, there was something about the fanciful, joyous, wide-eyed and oddly vulnerable beauty that tugged at him, when he didn't want to be tugged at.

"You could just ask her out, you know."

Sam jerked his gaze off the opening through the kitchen doors, where he'd been staring like an idiot at Angie, and faced Josephine, who calmly filled up his mug with fresh coffee. "What?"

"I said, you could just ask her out—"

"Yeah. I mean no."

"Don't tell me you're one of those." Josephine plopped her considerable frame next to Sam, with a large bowl of fruit and a paring knife. "One of those uncommittable types."

"It doesn't matter what I am when it comes to Angie."

"No?" Calmly Josephine started cutting fruit with the knife that looked sharp enough to cut through glass. "Why not? She not good enough for you?" She hefted the knife in her hand as she looked at him. "Maybe you ought to rethink that."

Sam looked at the knife, at the way she was wielding it, and lifted a brow of his own. "You threatening a cop, Josephine?"

"I'm threatening a man." Unapologetically, she reached for a cantaloupe. "Consider me a mother lion. Possessive and protective as hell."

"Not asking Angie out has nothing to do with her not being good enough. She is. She's…" Better than good enough, but he lifted his mug to his mouth to keep the thought to himself and burned his tongue for the effort.

"She'd go." Josephine continued to slice up the fruit. "If you asked her."

Sam sighed and put down the mug. Scalded tongue and all, he said, "I'm not interested in her that way."

"Then why are you hanging around here every morning?" Josephine raised a brow. "My coffee isn't that special."

"Actually, it is. And…" He risked one more look at Angie through the kitchen door, who was smiling at a man who had to be ninety years old.

"That's Eddie. He's been coming here for fifty years, through eight different owners, he's told me. He's nearly deaf and has arthritis pretty bad, but he's got all his faculties together. Watch. She'll keep talking to him and cut up his food at the same time so he doesn't have to work his fingers, and he'll never know what hit him."

Indeed, Angie shifted forward, set down a pot

of coffee and, with a sleight of hand, she cut up the man's food for him. All while smiling and chattering and keeping her eyes out for her other customers.

"She's been hurt," Josephine said into the silence. "By a man."

Damn it. "I don't want to know this."

"He wanted to change her. Make her into something she wasn't, and in the doing of that, took away most of her confidence. She'd deny it, of course, but it was the truth."

"Look, I'm just here to make sure—"

"That she's okay. Yeah, yeah, yeah. You don't want to know more, because you might realize the truth—"

"Josephine—"

"—that you care, too. That you know she's not quite as strong as she pretends to be. That you could hurt her."

"I am not going to hurt her. We're not together. Not in that way."

"Right. I forgot." Josephine got up and took away both the pot of coffee and his mug.

Apparently he was done here.

Chapter 5

Angie spent her free afternoons at the bookstore. There, in a lovely corner the owners had set up as a reading and study spot, she absorbed the books for her classes and daydreamed.

In between reading and fantasizing—which included far too much time spent on one Sam O'Brien—she chitchatted with the owners, George and Ellie Wilson. A couple in their mid-fifties, they'd put everything they had, including their retirement fund, into the store the year before, and were on pins and needles trying to work their way out of the red and into the black.

Ellie seemed to have a soft spot for Angie, and

always wanted to hear about her life. They'd talked about the holdup, the dramatic rescue, her life afterward, and seemed very supportive that she'd decided to take control of her destiny.

"So…has your cop asked you out yet?" Ellie asked during a lull in between customers.

"He's not *my* cop, but no, he hasn't asked me out. He's not going to." Angie wasn't sure whether she was relieved or disappointed.

Okay, she was disappointed.

"He sure stops by to see you a lot," Ellie noted casually.

"That's because of his work, that's all." She'd explained Sam's current case, and how she'd recognized his prime suspect, how she was determined to help him put the guy in jail.

"Oh, dear." Ellie came around the counter and took Angie's hand. "It's all about his work? That's it?"

Unfortunately. "Yes."

"So he's being difficult."

"Of course not."

"Isn't that just like a man. You know, you'd be better off to walk away. Police work can be dangerous."

"Oh, I'm sure I'm not in any danger."

"Just be safe, dear."

"I will, but—" She stopped when her cell phone rang. For a moment, her heart kicked in gear, thinking it might be Sam.

How ridiculous *that* would be.

Ellie patted Angie's hand and went off to see to another customer.

Angie looked down but didn't recognize the incoming call, and figured it for a sales pitch or a wrong number. "Hello?"

"Stop calling the cops."

The hair on the back of her neck rose at the gruff, unrecognizable voice. "Excuse me?"

"Back off, Angie, and stay there."

"What?" But she heard the telltale click and pulled the phone away from her ear to stare at it.

"Angie? You okay?" This from Ellie again, who was rushing through the aisle, looking busy, harassed and yet sweetly concerned. "You seem a little peaked."

"Oh, no. I'm fine." Angie managed a smile and a little wave. "Everything's just…fine."

With a nod, Ellie continued on, and Angie stood there for a moment, a strange and odd sense of unreality washing over her.

Back off, Angie, and stay there.

Definitely the message was for her. Oh boy. She sat back down, feeling a little shaky.

That her first instinct was to call Sam and let out all her fears really disturbed her.

Sam was not her friend. Not her sounding board. And if she needed a cop, she would call one. A different one.

Stop calling the cops.

She wouldn't do that. But Sam didn't want to be involved in her life, any more than she wanted him there. No. That was a lie. She did want him—as a friend, a lover.

But she had her pride.

And yet…this involved his case. It had to, because what else could it involve? With regret and a loud sigh, she broke down and dialed.

"O'Brien."

"Sam." She drew a deep breath. "Look, I—"

"I'm not available," came his recorded message. "Leave your name and number."

His machine. She waited for the beep. "Hi. It's me. Angie." Why did she sound like such a loser? "I received a prank phone call today and I'm pretty sure it's related to your case. So…call me. Bye."

Yep, loser. A loser who missed him. Grabbing her things, she let herself out of the store, thinking if she couldn't have Sam, an ice-cream sundae might just do.

* * *

Several hours later, as Angie sat in class learning fascinating things about the daily uses of algebra, she had a burning need to look at her cell phone.

She pulled it out of her purse, wondering how to bring up the list of calls she'd received. Reading the instructions would have helped.

Did she even still have them? Maybe the arrow button…

Dialed—911.

Hmm, that was her last call *out* on her cell phone, which had been when she'd seen Sam's suspect… days ago now.

"Uh…Angie? Earth to Angie, come in, Angie."

She jerked her head up to realize several things at once. First, the professor had apparently been addressing her for the past few moments. Second, the entire class was staring at her.

And third, every time she'd hit a button on her phone, it had beeped. Loudly.

With an apologetic smile, she slipped the phone back into her purse. "Sorry," she whispered, sinking into her seat.

With an exasperated look, the professor turned back to the board. Eventually people stopped staring at her.

And for the first time since class had started, Angie waited with baited breath for it to be finished, only to, on the way home, nearly drive into a pole when her cell phone rang again. She pulled over, lifting the phone close to her face where she could read the incoming number. Same as before. "Hello?" She hated the nerves that vibrated through her body, and forced herself to sound…not scared. *"Hello?"*

"I told you not to call the cops. Now *back off.*"

At that frightening, gruff voice in her ear, she instinctively cut off the call and dropped the phone into her purse as if it were a hot potato.

In spite of the cool evening, her palms were damp, her stomach lodged in her throat.

He knew she'd called Sam. How did he know?

Back off. What did that even mean? She wasn't a threat to anyone, she knew less than nothing… didn't she?

Slowly she pulled back out into traffic, driving through the night toward her apartment, where she'd call Sam again with the latest and probably sleep with every light on. So much for fearless. But she wouldn't run scared, she wouldn't.

Back off.

"Like hell," she muttered, downshifting with aggression. "Like hell."

* * *

Sam and Luke stood in front of a seedy, run-down apartment in downtown Los Angeles.

"No one's home," Luke said with disgust, turning away from the opened window they'd peered into. "Not that it matters, there's nothing much to see. Some lead that weasel Lou gave us."

"Well, he's not called a weasel for nothing." But Sam was disappointed, too. They'd spent countless hours searching through the student database at Pasadena City College for all the students with the first name of John. Incredibly, there hadn't been that many. Slowly but surely over the past week they'd worked their way through the list.

The guy who lived here, one of their "John's," had a mysterious background and an oddly far away location from the school. Seemed suspect.

But there was nothing to indicate this place was connected to their case, nothing to indicate anything at all except… Sam put his face back to the window and eyed the small stack of papers just on the inside, right within reach on a little desk directly beneath the glass.

He could reach them if he wanted. And he wanted. He looked at Luke, who shook his head.

Sam reached in anyway.

Luke sighed and promptly turned the other way. "Nice night."

"Yeah," Sam said, hitting the jackpot. "Really nice."

Luke whipped back. "How nice?"

"Well, we have an interesting receipt." Sam stared down at the bookstore receipt, from the very same bookstore Angie swore their suspect kept popping up at.

"Could be coincidence."

"I don't believe in coincidence."

"Me neither." Luke's eyes went hard, as did Sam's. They'd both been through far too much to trust anything to happenstance or fate. "Let's come back and talk to good old John when he's home sometime soon."

"Excellent idea."

On the way back to Pasadena, Sam called in for his messages, his heart stopping when he heard Angie's voice telling him she had a little problem.

At the details of that little problem, his heart started again, a heavy, unnatural beat. He called her cell phone, her work, her apartment. No answer.

And his feeling went from bad to worse.

God, he hated this, the worry factor. *Just work,* he told himself. *It's just work.*

Tell that to Dad, came a little voice inside his head. His father had lived work. And died work.

Sam had been only four when his father had been shot during a routine pull-over, but he'd made his vow to grow up and become a cop, too, even if his mother had been against it with every fiber of her being. Being on the force was all he'd ever wanted, *still* wanted, even when his mother objected to the point of asking him to walk right out of her life. Even when his wife had done the same, both unable or unwilling to deal with the danger and demands of the job that so consumed him.

Sam had learned to close off his heart for good, and told himself—never again.

It was a plan that had worked well, for the most part. He still called his mother on her birthday. Sometimes she even picked up. But she kept a careful distance, and Sam knew it was all she had to give him. Fair enough, he supposed, since he apparently had nothing to give her in return.

It didn't matter. He had his own life, and it was a life he loved. Everything was fine. Or had been until a certain bank incident.

Now Sam couldn't get his head on straight, and he knew whose fault that was.

Angie's.

"I'll give the paperwork twenty minutes," Luke

said when they got back to the station and their respective paper-ladened desks. "But then I'm outta here and on my way to a late, hot date."

"It's been a long time since you put a woman before duty."

"It's been a long time since I've wanted to." Luke looked Sam over solemnly. "You oughta think about doing the same, getting a life outside of this place."

"I've tried that before. And so have you."

"Maybe it's time to try again."

No, it wasn't. Luke was just currently being run by hormones. It'd pass, it always did.

Sam made himself as comfortable as he could on his hard chair with a cup of the worst coffee on the planet and looked at the piles of paperwork waiting on him.

No good. He couldn't concentrate. He bypassed the mess and reached for the newspaper from the day of the holdup. He looked at himself on the floor holding the most incredible woman, who was staring at him with stars in her eyes.

Not since the time he hadn't taken her seriously in his office had she looked at him with those stars in her eyes.

And now, terrifyingly enough, *he* was the one with stars in his eyes.

Just work, he reminded himself. Work would get him through.

But beautiful dark brown eyes kept his thoughts murky, and he kept his ears cocked for a return call from Angie, which clearly meant no matter what he wanted to believe about what was happening between them, this was far more than work.

Angie opened the door of her car and stared out into the night that suddenly seemed dark and yawning.

From where she stood, she couldn't see her front door. The path was covered by the yard she hadn't yet trimmed back. What looked charming and full of personality during the day, with all its color and vibrant growth, now seemed thick and unwelcoming.

Slowly she started up the path, thinking she shouldn't have just called Sam, she should have gone to the station.

After the last prank call on her way home, she'd decided to turn off her cell phone. Maybe that was like an ostrich putting her head in the sand, but it worked for her.

Someone seemed to think she knew more than she did. But she didn't, and surely this nervousness was nothing a good hot shower wouldn't cure.

Maybe by then, she'd have heard from Sam, and he'd calm her down. He could do that, with just his low, husky voice and sharp, piercing eyes that didn't miss a thing. He'd tell her if she was overreacting, whether she wanted to hear it or not.

Odd, how that could be soothing and a charge at the same time. He was an enigma, that man, no doubt there. The sexiest enigma she'd ever met.

She made it to the front door without event, and then inside, where she lit up the place like Christmas. Then she went into her bedroom and stripped out of her clothes, leaving them where they fell because it was already way past laundry day. She'd gather them tomorrow.

Tony had hated that habit. With him, everything had a place and had to be in it, at all times. Her happily cluttered apartment, with its plants scattered here and there, and mismatched throw rugs and shelves filled with books that were for reading not collecting drove him crazy.

Basically, *she* drove him crazy. And as a result, she'd begun to doubt herself. Her looks, her smarts, her everything, which had only led to hurt.

She hadn't imagined being happy without him, and yet she was happier now than she'd ever been.

Oddly enough, it was the holdup—the most terrifying moment in her life—that had taught her the life-changing lessons all in a flash.

When she thought of it that way, a good part of her nerves vanished. Relieved, she headed directly for the shower, where she stood for nearly half an hour under the spray of water.

Twice she imagined she heard something from the other side of the bathroom door and froze. And both times she ended up shaking her head at herself. She'd lived here for years, and no one had ever bothered her. Still, she poked her head from behind the curtain and glanced at the cell phone she'd placed on the counter. It was still off, damn it. which probably explained why Sam hadn't called her back. But at least it was right there if she needed it, with 911 already programmed in.

The shower felt heavenly, both the tingle of water on her skin and the easing of her mind. For a moment, loose and relaxed, she wished she had a man with her in the water. Sam. Sam with slow, knowing hands and a body hungry for hers.

But that was a physical need and could be ignored. Still his face flickered in her mind, and the need tightened because she was quite certain when he set his mind to something, say making love, he'd do it right.

That thought made her quiver, but the water

slowly turned less warm, then downright chilly. Finally she shut it off, purposely ignoring the deep yearning. It was just that she hadn't had any sort of physical relationship since Tony, she told herself, and that had been nearly a year now.

A year without sex. She needed to remedy that.

Later. For now, sleep, and lots of it. She stepped out of the shower and wrapped herself in the lone towel hanging on the rack.

Definitely laundry day tomorrow. Without a towel for her dripping hair, she combed it back from her face and opened the bathroom door.

All the steam escaped, and at first she couldn't see. As the mist dissipated, two things hit her at once. First, the answering machine on her nightstand was blinking like crazy, and she realized she'd forgotten to listen to the messages when she'd gotten home.

But it was the second thing that rendered her a speechless, trembling mass of fear.

Her place had been ransacked. Blankets, pillows and sheets had been tossed everywhere, her dresser and closet drawers opened and dumped.

Shock immobilized her. She stood in the doorway of the bathroom, water from her hair dripping down her shoulders and back, still clinging to the towel wrapped around her. Her first instinct was to run back into the bathroom and lock the door. But that wouldn't do her any good as the door didn't lock—it never had.

Grabbing the cell phone, she pushed on the power button and stood in indecision for one horrifying second.

Was she alone?

Was someone even now listening to her panicked breathing, just waiting to make their move?

Oh, God. This couldn't be happening, not again. She didn't want to die in a towel, any more than she had wanted to die in a bank robbery.

Quietly as she could, she backed into the bathroom, pulling the door closed, wincing as it squeaked, desperately wishing she'd bothered to have the lock fixed as she'd been meaning to do for months.

Somehow she found the wits to crank back on the shower, which would hopefully muffle the sound of her voice. But because it was icy water now, not a drop of hot left, she left it running out of the tub spout as she hopped in and shut the curtain, crouching as far back as she could to avoid the spray.

She looked down at her cell phone and hoped to God she couldn't get electrocuted while operating it with her feet in the water. She hit redial, a number she was becoming unfortunately familiar with, and waited with baited breath to be attacked before the dispatcher came on.

But she got Sam.

He answered on the first ring with, "Where the hell have you been?" making her realize 911 hadn't been the last call she'd made after all.

It had been Sam's cell phone.

She let out a shaky laugh, her feet frozen from the water running over them, her little towel that didn't cover enough chilled skin slipping. "I need you," she whispered.

She hadn't meant to say that. In a million years she wouldn't have planned to say it.

"I've been trying to call you," he said right over her. "About those prank calls—"

"Sam." She gripped the phone tight and shuddered. "Did you hear me? I need you. I...really need you. Right now."

Utter silence. Then in a voice gone soft and regretful, he said, "Angie, you know we can't. I'm a cop, and you're a part of the job, and—"

Okay, damn it, she was not going to cry. So he'd misunderstood. So he'd rejected her out of hand. She'd known he would. "I mean someone broke into my apartment, Sam."

"Where are you now?"

"Here."

"Here where, Angie?" Now his voice was calm, alert. In control.

And very professional.

"In my apartment."

He swore. Very unprofessionally.

And oddly enough, that soothed her more than anything else could have.

"Get out of there, now."

She looked down at her very undressed self and nearly let out a hysterical laugh. "I...can't."

"Angie, listen to me very carefully. Arm yourself with something."

"Arm myself?"

"A vase. A golf club. Something."

She peeked out the shower curtain and saw a can of hairspray, which she clutched to her chest. "Got it."

"Did you call—"

"Nine-one-one. They're next on my list."

"I'll do it. Hang tight. I'm on my way."

Hang tight. Hanging tight. Knees knocking together, she sank to her knees on the floor of the tub and waited.

Chapter 6

I need you.

Those three little words tore at Sam as he raced to Angie's apartment. Why the hell hadn't he just gone over there when he'd gotten her earlier message? That she hadn't answered her phone shouldn't have stopped him.

That she scared him shouldn't have stopped him.

He drove faster. He was a professional, and as a professional he willingly headed into situations similar to this all the time. It was his job.

But the cool, calm, professional cop he was inside

had vanished and been replaced by a man—a terrified, protective, angry man he hardly recognized.

Why had this happened to Angie, a woman who deserved hearts and flowers and a white picket fence, not this sheer terror?

Damn it, she'd already been hurt. Josephine had told him that much. Hurt by a man who'd tried to mold her into his idea of the perfect woman.

How could someone do that to the vibrant, sweet, open Angie?

Shame furled in his belly as he remembered his first impression of her. Scattered. Flighty. Naive.

She wasn't any of those things.

Please don't let her be hurt, he prayed, and vowed right then and there to never add to that hurt of hers. And it wasn't ego that told him he could do exactly that. Even he couldn't deny there was something…undeniable between them.

That he'd lost all perspective when it came to her didn't escape him. He was a man darkly driven and intensely private. He was a man who had no right to be thinking about hearts and flowers and a white picket fence.

He was a cop, through and through, and he'd learned the hard way through his mother, then his ex-wife, that no one could get close to him.

No one ever would.

How many times had he heard that cops didn't make good relationship material?

Yes, there was more to life than work, he knew this, but he also knew it wasn't worth the headache.

God, *please,* let her be okay.

Getting to her place was the longest four minutes in history, but finally he came around the last corner to her building.

Her entire apartment was ablaze with lights. And no squad car out front, which meant, despite his call to dispatch, she was still alone inside.

Her front door was ajar. Pulling his gun, he pushed the door all the way open.

Her bookshelf had been dumped, her television and portable CD player broken on the floor. And despite the fact he could hear water running somewhere, there was no sign of life. "Angie?"

From the small living room he could see into the even smaller kitchen. The cupboards had been opened, emptied. The plants in hand-painted ceramic bins had been purposely slammed to the floor and lay broken among her dishes and glasses.

He'd seen enough to know that someone had tried to scare her, and undoubtedly it had worked.

Silent now, with terror chasing chills along his

spine, he headed down the hall. Bedroom trashed. And empty.

The bathroom door was shut, beyond which he could hear running water. With a palm to the door, he shoved it open, gun ready.

The small room was the only one in the house not messed with. The tub curtain was drawn closed, which was odd, given that he could hear the spout running behind it.

Battle ready, he yanked the curtain open and steadied his gun.

Only to drop it to his side a split second later with a soft, harsh oath. "Angie."

She was down in the far corner of the tub, eyes wide as saucers. "I've been waiting for you."

His heart all but cracked as he reached in and turned off the water. Ice-cold. Gently he pulled her out of the tub and ran his hands down her frozen arms. He could hardly breathe. "Are you hurt?"

She shook her head.

"Talk to me." Cupping her face, he tilted it up. *"Are you hurt?"*

"N-no."

Thank God. He struggled for his professionalism, barely found it. "You're cold." He went and grabbed the comforter off her bed, then pulled it around her.

"I got prank calls."

"What did they say?"

"Mostly that I'm to stop calling the cops."

He went still. "Which you didn't do."

"Nope."

"So this was to scare you. What else did he say?"

"Back off." She managed a wry half smile. "I get the distinct impression I've hurt your suspect's feelings." She rubbed her forehead as if her head hurt.

He resisted, barely, the urge to haul her close. "Tell me what happened tonight."

She sighed and looked around as if she was still surprised to see the mess. "I came home from class, let myself in and…" She lifted a shoulder and turned away.

"You what?"

"This and that…you know, ever since the holdup, I've…had a little trouble sleeping."

His gut clenched, thinking of her here. All alone. Frightened.

"I've been flipping on all the lights at night. That's the first thing I did tonight."

"There's no shame in that," he said to her back.

"Yeah." Then she let out a little laugh at herself that tore at him, and she pulled the comforter tighter around her. "Then I came into my bedroom and…"

He waited but she didn't say anything else. "Angie? You what?"

She opened her mouth, then closed it. A tinge of embarrassment crept over her face. "I…stripped off my clothes and got into the shower." She studied her toes. "Do you think they saw me?"

Damn it. "Angie—"

"No. Never mind." She wrapped her arms around herself. "It doesn't matter. It's over, right?"

"That's right," he said gently, stepping closer. "It's over." And he would do everything in his power to make sure it stayed over. "What happened next?"

"I stayed in the shower for a really long time." She lifted her shoulder again. "I sang. Probably scared whoever it was to death, as I'm pretty much tone-deaf."

Sam couldn't imagine anything about her scaring anyone.

Except him, of course. He was scared to death of her.

"When I got out," she continued, "the place had been all messed up."

"But you never saw anyone? Heard anything?"

"No." She bit her lower lip, which started to tremble.

Oh, God, the tremble.

Tears would be next. "Angie—"

Without another word, she dropped the comforter and went straight into the arms he hadn't realized he'd held out. She burrowed close, pressing her icy nose into the crook of his neck, slipping her arms around his waist, fitting against him as if she'd been made for him.

His heart, the one he'd thought impenetrable as stone, squeezed hard. Her hair was wet. Dripping all over him, in fact. And she wore only a towel. Just a little scrap of material. She'd been in the shower, at her most vulnerable. At the thought of what could have happened to her, helpless rage filled him, and he found his arms tightening around her in a way they wouldn't have done around any other victim.

Against his neck, she swallowed hard. "When I came out, I worried I wasn't alone, that…" She shuddered and didn't go on, but she didn't need to.

He bent his head, put his mouth to her temple. "It's okay now." This was no regular victim, this was Angie. She was different, and she had been from the very first moment he'd laid eyes on her. He didn't think of her as part of the job, no matter how much he wished he could relegate her to that part of his mind. "We're alone. It's all right now."

"I know." She sniffed but didn't pull away. "I'm fine. I can handle this."

Another sniff sounded.

Ah, hell. "Angie…"

"No, really. I'm okay." But her voice cracked, and she was shaking like a damn blender. "I'm not going…to fall apart."

"Of course you're not," he said, willing it to be true.

"It's just that…I wanted excitement in my life, you know?" She let out a little hiccup. "But I had something else in mind. Like learning to teach."

"It's okay," he whispered, rubbing his jaw over her hair, wondering who was comforting whom. Because somehow, she'd wormed her way into his heart despite his resolve.

Not good.

In fact, it was really bad. Bad timing. Bad form. Bad everything.

In his experience, women fell into two categories: the kind who couldn't handle his job—his mother and his ex-wife, for example. And then there were the danger junkies, the woman who wanted a rush of edgy adrenaline to excite their lives.

He didn't want to think of Angie as a danger junkie, since he understood she was flexing her wings for the first time. She would never use him that way.

As for his job and all that entailed, it didn't seem to faze her, but he knew, given enough time, it sure as hell would. It fazed everyone sooner or later.

Then her fingers found the skin at the back of his neck. Just a little stroke that woke up every nerve in his body.

Her other hand lay trustingly on his chest.

As he looked down at her fingers, at her, everything within him stilled. He was attracted to her, on some deep level he couldn't ignore no matter how he tried.

And he was responsible for her—this uninhibited, sparkly-as-hell woman who was so damn warm and thrilled with her new lease on life it almost hurt to even look at her.

The truth was simple: he cared, far more than he wanted to.

Talk about terror.

Angie didn't know how long they stood like that, wrapped together, her nearly nude body to his fully clothed one. "Sam?"

"Yeah?"

She swallowed hard and tried to put the words

in the right order. "Thank you for coming. I meant to call 911 but…"

It didn't say much for her newfound independence that she'd called him instead, but she figured she was allowed to lean on someone once in a while.

And he certainly had the strength to be leaned on. He had it in spades. God, the way he'd arrived, like the cavalry, all magnificent and edgy-looking, until he'd found her huddled in the bathtub. Then he'd gone so gentle, so…tender. She liked that side of him.

Too much.

"I don't want to be thanked for this."

Oh, yes, his voice was calm and assuring, but even Sam couldn't hide his eyes, which were filled with heat and a fierce, urgent concern.

That alone warmed her toward him in a way she doubted he'd understand. It hadn't been often in her life someone had felt those things for her. She liked it, the fierce concern. She liked it a lot. She also liked the heat. It did something to her insides, made her want to…glow. She'd always shied away from any serious emotional attachments, even with Tony. It made it easier when she didn't live up to their expectations.

But she wasn't the same person anymore. She wanted more for herself. So much more. Living life to the fullest meant no more pretending her yearnings didn't exist.

Sam had probably never in his life had such thoughts. He was strong. His own man. If he wanted something, he went after it, and she admired that. "Are you always so tough?" she wondered softly. "So in control?"

He pulled back, looked at her. "I like to be in control."

"But why?" She wanted to be distracted, and there could be no better one than learning about this man. "What made you that way?"

He lifted a broad shoulder. "Genes."

"Your dad?"

"Actually, my mom. She's the master of control. She's...never forgiven me for being a cop."

"Never?"

"Never. But that's what I am, Angie." He shocked her by lifting a big hand and wrapping a wet tendril of her hair around his finger. "That's who I am." His touch made her want to close her eyes. His voice made her want to burrow back against him. "By definition alone," he said very, very quietly, "control is everything."

"But you're also a man." A man who was touching her, very lightly, very tenderly. Her insides did a funny dance, and as if he could read his thoughts, his eyes flared at the knowledge there.

"A cop first," he said, his voice low. Rough. "Don't confuse it."

"I won't, I couldn't." She entwined her fingers through the silky hair at the back of his neck. "You're a cop through and through, I can see that. I accept that."

"I doubt it."

"It's true." But she could see she'd have to prove that much to him. Maybe he'd been hurt. Betrayed. She had no way of knowing, much as she wanted to. "But this rigid control…this holding back… Sam, life can't be lived to its fullest that way. It just can't."

"I don't hold back."

But that's just what he'd done, from the very first with her. His mouth was so close to hers. Just a shiver, a single breath, and they'd be connected. "Don't you?" she whispered.

He stared down at her mouth.

Oh yes, she had his attention now. Not as a victim. Or a responsibility. But as a woman. "I know how hard it is. Believe me, Sam, I know how hard it is to let go, because until recently, I've lived most of my life denying my own ambitions, my own happiness. It was easier to do so than to face them. Which is really the same as all this rigid control you've got, don't you see?" Her throat felt tight. "I've learned it's much more fulfilling to be a butterfly than a caterpillar. I'm only guessing, because I'm still really new at this, but I know it's going to be great."

Still staring at her, he let out one long breath. "You'll make a great butterfly, Angie. You will. You were made for it. But for me...that sort of thing doesn't work. Control does."

"And toughness."

"And toughness," he agreed with a hint of a smile. He dropped his hand from her hair. "It's how I want to be. No exceptions."

"But—"

He touched her again, put a finger to her lips. "No exceptions," he repeated.

She didn't want to look at him, not when she knew her heart was right there in her eyes for him to see. He'd hate that, so she did the first thing that came to her. She closed her eyes and pressed her face back against his throat.

He smelled so good. Like soap and heat and man. And she remembered her new vow, not to let anything stop her from what she wanted, not ever again.

So she was scared, so what? Fear wouldn't stop

her either, and she leaned into Sam's heat and strength, letting it surround her.

His arms surrounded her, too, probably because he thought she needed more comfort, but that's not what she wanted at all.

Not from him.

So she lifted her head, found his mouth with hers and showed him what she *did* want.

For one long heartbeat, he froze. Very lightly she touched the corner of his mouth with her tongue, then the other corner, and with a low, rough groan, he dragged her closer, whispered her name hoarsely and opened to her.

It was a kiss like nothing she'd ever known. She felt like she was drowning in him, in the pleasure and heat and need of it.

But from the window came the sound of one car pulling up, then another. Telltale blue and red lights flashed, slashing through the room.

Angie's reinforcements had come, which meant this little interlude, the most amazing she'd ever had, was over.

Chapter 7

An hour later, the excitement was over. The police were tracking the prank calls. They'd dusted for prints. They'd made a report. They'd left.

All that remained now was for Angie to wait until they made sense of what had happened.

Normally Sam felt only impatience for the victim who couldn't do that. Now, suddenly, he felt his own vicious impatience with the system that required her to hang tight like a sitting duck and wait it out.

Angie stood in front of her living room window, staring out into the dark night. She'd put on a tank top and a pair of sweatpants that had seen better days. Faded and nearly threadbare, he could have sworn a patch low on her very lovely behind had nearly worn through, showing him a hint of bare flesh.

Suddenly all he could think about was whether she had anything on beneath, and if not…

Sam shook his head and purposely shifted his gaze upward, to her narrow, tense shoulders, and the way she had her arms wrapped around herself as if she had no one but her own company for comfort.

Moving forward, he put his hands on her shoulders to shift her away from the window, wanting to bring her farther into the room, but at the touch of his fingers, she jerked.

"Hey, hey," he said softly, lifting his hands from her, smiling easily as she whipped around, eyes wide, breath hitching. "Just me."

"Yeah." Again her own arms snaked around her waist. "I knew that." She looked around. "So…I guess you're going to go now, too, right?"

"I'd rather you let me call someone, a friend… anyone."

"No, I'm fine. Thanks." But her smile didn't reach her eyes.

"Angie—"

"Really." She turned toward the front door. A not-so-subtle invitation for him to go. "Good night."

No reason for him to feel that he had a vise on

his heart, just because she was trying to be so brave, so tough, when any idiot could see it was all for show.

She opened the front door.

He stepped toward it. At his side, she stood there waiting, her head bowed so he couldn't see her face, her eyes.

Just go, O'Brien. Walk away.

He almost did it. Started to pass her, but then before he could think, he was reaching out, lifting her chin with his fingers, using his other hand to gently tuck a strand of hair behind her ear. "I can't leave you like this."

"I won't be someone's burden."

"I didn't mean it like that."

She took a deep breath and stepped back from his touch. "Then how did you mean it?"

His mind blanked.

At his lack of response, she turned away. "I'm sorry, never mind. But thanks again for coming," she added with extreme politeness.

"Go," she whispered, when he stood there.

Yeah, he should go, because he knew, just as she did, that if he stayed...

"*Please*, Sam."

He even lifted his foot to take the last step out of her door. Right out of her life.

But he set it back down again, tugged her clear from the door and shut it.

"Sam—"

"I'm not leaving you here alone, damn it, don't ask me to."

"But…" She blinked a little uncertainly. "Really?"

"Yeah."

Without another word, she threw her arms around his neck and hugged him, plastered her warm, curvy body to his.

She probably meant to soften him, or to simply comfort herself, but the connection actually had the opposite effect. As his body tightened in a mixture of arousal and protective affection, he pulled her close and let himself be sucked into the surge of pleasure.

It destroyed him, this terrible need he had to keep her safe, far more than the lust did.

The lust he expected. The lust was normal.

But the other…

How in the hell was this happening?

"Thank you," she whispered against him. He pressed his face to the warm skin of her neck, breathing in her fresh scent, thanking God she was really okay, that nothing had happened to her. He pressed his mouth to the tender curve of her neck, inhaling deeply of her when she closed her eyes and tipped her head, allowing him better access. "Angie," he murmured.

"Shh." Her hands cupped his jaw, brought his mouth back to hers, which was blindingly seeking… and when their lips touched, they both sighed. Like a coming-home sort of sigh, and he decided to worry about it later, because he couldn't think of anything except how she felt against him, whole and safe in his arms, pressed against his aching flesh.

Her hands moved over his shoulders, restlessly over his back and up his chest. This wasn't just a kiss. He knew this, even in his befuddled state. Then she deepened the connection, her tongue shyly sliding to his in an age-old rhythm that had him growling low in his throat and tugging her even closer. His hands moved, too, and he wasn't too far gone to know he should be thankful she'd put on clothes, because he didn't know if he could have resisted Angie in nothing more than a small, damp towel.

Then her hands slid beneath the hem of his shirt, gliding over the bare skin of his back, and God help him, but he did the same. His fingers danced over the back hook of her bra, dallied, played…

"Sam."

The way she said his name, on a sigh of breath

that could have been a plea, a prayer, a curse…
But her mouth came back to his—insisting, needy,
hungry, and he gave her all he had, which was far
more than he'd known he had. Tasting, sucking,
nibbling—by the time they broke apart, breathless,
he couldn't have put a thought together to save his
life.

Then he was kissing her again, and she was
kissing him back, and he wasn't worried about
breathing, because nothing mattered more than this.
Her hands slid up his bare belly now, her fingers
gliding over his chest, his nipples, which actually
hardened beneath her touch and elicited another
deep-throated growl from him.

At the sound, she pulled back slightly, her mouth
wet and already swollen, her eyes slumberous but
just with a twinge of anxiety. "You…don't like
that?"

"No. *Yes*." What was he doing? "Don't stop," he
said in a strangled voice.

"Oh, good, because I was hoping…" Then she
covered his hands with hers, and gently but inex-
orably moved them off her hips, over her ribs, then
even higher, until the tips of his fingers were just
touching the bottom curves of her breasts.

He closed his eyes and concentrated on breathing.

"Sam," she whispered in that voice again, the

one thready with desire and need, and there was no way he could resist her sweet plea, no way he wanted to.

She fit perfectly in his palms, one sweet, curved breast in each, and as she let out a choppy breath, he stroked his thumbs over her satin-covered nipples, groaning at the feel of them tightening against his touch.

Her head fell back against the front door. Her hair was free, flowing over her shoulders, a strand of it clinging to the stubble of his jaw. Her eyes were closed, her breath coming in little pants as he rasped his fingers over her again and again. Her mouth fell open a little, as if she needed it open to simply breathe. Her skin glowed damp and rosy. And against his, her hips arched, rubbing the neediest part of her over the neediest part of him.

He didn't have a condom. That thought stopped him cold, as did his second, and far more devastating one...she was not the sort of woman who could separate sex and love. For her the two would come together.

Not for him.

Not ever for him.

This shouldn't happen. This couldn't happen, but before he pulled back, she did. She put a finger to his lips and sighed as she opened her eyes. "I'm sorry." She met his gaze and slowly shook her head. "I don't want to stop. God, I don't want to. But…"

"Protection." He had to clear his rough throat. "I know."

"No. Not that." Her smile was so many things— sweet, sad, regretful, as she pulled her hands from beneath his shirt, leaving him feeling…cold. "This isn't something I…" Her cheeks went a little red, further endearing her to him. "I don't do this lightly, you see, and—"

"Angie, I know. I—"

"Please. Let me finish. I want to make love with you. I want to because I think we could really have something. You're smart and wonderful and…" Her blush deepened. "And I think you're really sexy. But I don't want to be with someone who doesn't feel the same. I want you to respect me. I mean me as me."

When he opened his mouth, she put her fingers back on his lips. "I need someone who can see me for what I really am on the inside, not just the… well, you know, the pesky waitress." She drew a deep breath and straightened her shirt. "So this is a bad idea, no matter how much I want you."

He was the biggest jerk he knew. "Angie… God. I never meant to make you feel—"

"I know." She focused her dark eyes on his. "But

let's be honest, okay? I'm a big old pain in your butt half the time. We both know that."

He winced, dragged his hands down his face, and turned to look at her again. "I'm an ass. I really am. Know that right now. I like to keep people at arm's length. I mean, I really like that, Angie, and you're pretty impossible to keep that way."

"I know, I'm s—"

"Don't apologize. Don't. It's who you are. And no matter how I snap or growl at you, don't ever think I don't like or respect you, all right? I just…"

"Don't like to like me?"

That tore a smile out of him. "Yeah. Something like that. Look, my own mother doesn't understand me. I don't expect you to, either."

"Being a cop is who you are, Sam. I get that. I'm not like your mother. Don't you two ever talk about it?"

He blew out a breath. "No."

"Maybe you should."

"We never talk. Period."

Her eyes went soft. "Does she live near here?"

"She's a librarian here in town."

"At the library right across the street from your station?"

"Yeah. But we don't run in the same circles. Not

everything can be fixed by some sort of epiphany, Angie."

He was talking about the holdup. How she'd made the conscious effort to change her life because of it. "I know." She just thought it so wrong. She took one good look at the magnificent man in front of her and wondered who'd want to walk away from him.

Not her.

His hair was all messy, his shirt slightly askance. *She'd done that,* she realized with a good shock. She'd nearly devoured him.

And him her.

Stopping had been one of the hardest things she'd ever done, but even she had her pride. Sam, incredible kisser and amazing man that he was, was not the man for her. He never would be.

But he was still looking at her as if he wanted to gobble her up for dinner, and it was making her knees quiver. "I haven't made the wisest of choices with men before. And last time, I sort of ended up…"

"Hurt." He grimaced. "I know. Josephine told me. Right before she threatened to kill me with her paring knife if I did the same."

"She…threatened you?"

"Yeah. She's—"

"Fearless," she said with him, then laughed while he went very serious.

"You're different," he said quietly. "You...know me."

"I do."

He stepped close to her again, so close she could see the dance of light in his eyes, and the beginning hint of a five-o'clock shadow on his jaw.

"So tell me," he said very quietly. "What sort of lowlife could ever hurt you?"

"Oh. That." She lifted a shoulder. "Long story."

"Tell me."

"Well...Tony's an assistant district attorney." And another whose unrealistic expectations she'd avoided. "He's smart. Strong. The perfect guy, everyone always tells me. I should have done whatever I could to keep him. But he didn't like my clothes, my job, or anything about me other than I suited his lifestyle because I was easy-going. I didn't rock the boat. And it was true, Sam. I wanted to make him happy. I really wanted that."

"And then he left you." He touched her cheek. "He was an idiot, Angie."

She shook her head. "You think he left me."

"Forget him."

"No, wait. You really think that." A little mirthless laugh escaped her. "You know, that's what everyone assumes. Which means I'm pretty pathetic in people's eyes." She looked up at him, her first spurt of temper feeling really, really good. "Tony left poor Angie. She'll never recover. How could she from losing a perfect man like that?"

She knew her eyes were suspiciously wet when she stabbed her finger into his chest and didn't care. "Well, guess what, Sam? I have *some* pride, at least. *I* left *him*."

She strode away from him rather than do something tempting, like start a fight he didn't deserve. But her body was humming, yearning, and she knew it was a hunger only Sam could fulfill, and that it wasn't going to happen. Which left her entitled to her grumpiness. "I'm not that same woman who'd go on status quo rather than face the truth. I wasn't living. I was existing."

"Angie…"

She kept walking, and since her apartment just wasn't that big, she was at the end of the hallway with nowhere to go but the bathroom or bedroom, inside of three seconds.

"Angie."

The bathroom, she decided. Good protection. Not for her, but for Sam, whom she still had the most terrible urge to plaster herself against.

"Hey, wait up." And then his foot was in the door, holding it open when she tried to slam it in his face.

"While I'm thrilled you've changed your life," he said, muscling his way in with ease. "I'm a little confused."

"You're confused?" This entire evening had been a bad nightmare. The break-in. Calling Sam—why had she called him? And then him finding her in her little pathetic huddle in the tub. She was stronger than that. "I have no idea what's happening to me," she said, feeling baffled.

"You need rest."

"No." She said what was really bothering her. "Sam, I don't want to die and not have really lived."

"You're not going to die."

"We all die. I enrolled in college. It's what I've always wanted."

"Okay. College is good."

"I don't intend to back off when it comes to your suspect."

"Angie—"

"I don't," she repeated firmly.

"Yeah." He moved in closer, let out a sigh and gently slid his arms around her for a hug that was shockingly welcome. "I already knew that."

When she set her head on his shoulder, he sighed again. "I'm sleeping on your couch."

"That's not necessary."

"I think it is."

"I'm fine."

"You're a horrible liar."

"I'll turn on all the lights. No biggee."

"I'm staying," he said, and this time he put his finger on her lips. "Don't argue with me."

She wrapped her fingers around his wrist. "I imagine not many would dare."

"You would."

"I'll try to restrain myself. So…you're sleeping here." When she spoke, her lips slid over his fingers.

Electrified, they both shivered.

"Yeah," he said. "On—"

"The couch," she finished for him. "You've mentioned."

"Just do me a favor. Don't come out in the morning in your towel. I'm going to do my damnedest to act like the professional I am."

Chapter 8

They cleaned up the apartment a little. Then Sam spent a long night on the couch, staring at Angie's living room ceiling, wondering what she was doing in her bed, wondering what she was wearing, how she looked… It was so damn juvenile.

Determined to think of something else, anything else, he flipped over…and fell off the couch. He spent some time swearing, before climbing back up and trying again. Tossing restlessly, he finally napped.

He rose at dawn. He crept down the hall and stared at Angie's closed door, his hand on the handle before he got a grip on himself and turned away.

In the kitchen, he grabbed a pad and pencil, then stared at them, wondering what to say.

That he needed to get out before he saw her rumpled and sexy from sleep? That he didn't know how long he could resist the temptation, no matter how good his intentions?

He finally settled on one brief line, telling her to call if she needed him, and that he'd be in touch. Then he left, without looking back.

Luke was waiting for Sam in his office, halfway through a chocolate doughnut and a large cup of black coffee. "Tried calling your place this morning," he said.

"Didn't hear the phone." Sam dug into the box of doughnuts and grabbed the spare cup of coffee.

Luke waited until he'd gulped a substantial sip of the really terrible but powerfully caffeinated brew. "Hard to hear the phone when you're wrapped around a woman."

In the middle of a swallow, Sam choked.

Luke set down his doughnut to smack Sam on the back. "Didn't mean to nearly kill you."

"I wasn't wrapped around a woman," he managed when he could get air down his burned windpipe. "I was at Angie's."

Luke lifted a brow.

"She was scared." Sam stared down at the jelly doughnut in his hand and scowled. "So I stayed, damn it."

"Then why are you still so uptight?"

"I slept on the couch."

"Ah." Luke, damn him, grinned at that. "What was wrong with her bed?"

"It's not like that between us."

"Uh-huh."

"It's not."

"Fool yourself if you want to, buddy, but you can't fool me."

Sam pointed to the door. "Don't you have anything better to do?"

"Sure." Luke tossed him a file. "The calls made to Angie's cell? All from a payphone across the street from her work."

Sam stared at him as that sank in. "Or across from the bookstore."

"Or the bookstore," Luke agreed with a nod. "Tied into our case then, you're thinking?"

"Oh, yeah. God knows, she's made herself visible enough. She's told people she recognized a suspect, that she's hoping to see him again. And with her place being trashed last night…"

"She wasn't hurt?"

"No." He swore softly and shoved his fingers

through his hair. "Nothing was stolen either. So were they searching for something or…?"

"Trying to scare her."

They'd been finishing each other's sentences for years. Hell, no one else could. Not their families, not their lovers—

But Angie could.

Not anxious to follow up that thought, Sam headed toward the door. "Let's go visit our John again."

"Right behind you."

John was a tall, wiry, spectacled twenty-year-old with a sweet smile that faded fast when Sam and Luke flashed their badges.

"Dude…I paid my tickets."

"This isn't about your tickets," Luke said. "A little birdie told us you knew something about getting new IDs."

John's expression went blank.

Sam rolled his eyes. "And I suppose you don't recognize this guy." He showed him the composite drawing of their suspect.

"Never seen him."

"Okay, let's try this," Sam said. "Where were you last night at approximately ten o'clock?"

John paled. "Here. Right here."

"Wrong," Sam said. "*We* were here, and you weren't."

"Okay, I was on my way here."

"Got a witness?"

Now he went a little green. "Do I need an attorney?"

"You tell us," Luke said. But he smiled easily. "Tell you what, John. Just answer a few questions and we'll go away. Fair enough?"

"Uh…" John divided an uneasy glance between the two men standing before him, one smiling nicely, one still as death. "Okay."

"You're a student at P.C.C., right?"

John nodded.

"That's good, really good," Luke said. "So…why do you live so far from campus?"

"Money," John said. "My parents own this building. They let me stay here rent free as long as I'm going to school."

"And last night you were…where?" Sam raised one brow while he waited, not exactly the same picture of patience as Luke.

"I…can't say."

"John, John, John…" Luke tsked. "That's not good."

"Want to go to jail, John?" Sam asked.

"No." The kid put his forehead to the doorjamb and closed his eyes. "I was with…"

"Just spit it out."

"Jeremy."

"Jeremy," Sam repeated carefully.

"My…boyfriend." John squeezed his eyes tighter. "You're not going to, like, make me tell anyone else, right? My parents don't know yet."

"We'll need a place to reach Jeremy," Sam said. "If you're telling the truth, it won't go further."

John lifted his head. "I'm telling the truth. I wish my roommate had been with us to verify everything, but he's out of town. So what's this about anyway?"

"Roommate?" Sam asked, getting very interested. "What roommate?"

"John? He's out of town, but due back tomorrow."

"You're both named John?" Sam asked, looking at Luke. "Well, isn't that interesting."

Remarkably, Angie woke with a tentative surge in her sunken spirits. Lying in bed, studying the dance of early-morning sunlight playing across her ceiling, she decided she wouldn't let the break-in keep her down.

In fact, she'd do with it just as she'd done with

the holdup. Use it to feed her strength and newfound determination.

And she would see this through. Obviously, she'd gotten to someone, and she didn't care. She wouldn't be frightened away from seeing justice served, not if she could help.

And then there was what had come after the break-in. The kiss. The amazing, brain-cell-destroying, bone-melting kiss.

And the way Sam had touched her…oh, boy. There was going to be some trouble resisting him, that was certain. Especially since he cared for her. No one could have looked at her as he had and not cared deeply. But it wasn't going to work, because he'd never let her in, not really. And she couldn't settle for less.

Was Sam still asleep on her couch? Lord, she hoped so. She wanted a chance to stare at all the long, lean, tough masculinity without him knowing. She wanted to drink in her fill.

And then walk away.

That part would be hard, but she was a grown up. She could do it. Tiptoeing into the living room, she was breathless already, and she hadn't even gotten a look at him yet.

She hoped he slept in the nude.

At that thought, she had to laugh at herself. Then sighed in disappointment at the empty couch.

She saw the note and sighed again.

Call if you need me. I'll be in touch.

Sam

Hmm, sounded like a promise. Too bad he was a man who didn't make them.

Josephine was waiting in the kitchen when Angie finally arrived. "You look pretty good for a woman whose apartment was broken into last night."

"How did you hear about last night?"

"The hunk called for you."

Angie set down her purse, picked up her apron and pretended her heart hadn't picked up speed. "Hunk?"

"Oh yeah." Josephine waved a wooden spoon. "Tell me everything, starting from the beginning."

"Sam called here for me?"

"You got another hunk sniffing around I don't know about?"

Angie leaned back against the refrigerator and tried to decide how she felt about Sam leaving before she woke, and then calling her. "He is pretty hunky, isn't he."

"He wanted to make sure you got here okay, so call him back."

"Yes, I will. But it's not going to be like that between us."

"Of course it is. He looks at you." Josephine fanned herself. "I mean *really* looks at you."

"Only because, for the most part, I drive him insane."

"For the most part?" Josephine looked very curious. "And what do you do when you're not driving him insane?"

Kiss him until I can't remember my name. "Oh, stop looking at me like that."

"Well, someone has to." Josephine came close, cupped Angie's face in her big hands. "Honestly, honey, I thought you were stronger than that. But the truth is, you still don't believe in yourself."

"I *do* believe in myself. So much that I want more for myself this time around. I want respect, Josephine. Affection." She sighed. "Love."

"So?" Josephine lifted her hands. "Go get it."

If only it was that simple. But with Sam, it wouldn't be. He'd been through too much, seen too much. He'd made up his mind not to open his heart, and though she could almost understand why, after all he'd been through, she also knew nothing she could do or say would change anything. "He doesn't have it to give. We're just…friends."

"Friends don't keep stopping by for coffee and then stare at you when you're not staring at him."

"He comes here because I keep seeing his suspect. That's all."

"Uh-huh."

"It is." Angie peered out the window and studied the alley, as she did every morning, wondering if she would see the guy yet again. Wondering if Ellie or George had seen him since she'd gone over there and asked them to keep their eyes open. "So stop matchmaking."

"Over my dead body," Josephine muttered beneath her breath when Angie went into the dining room to take orders. "Over my dead body."

Other than the fact that Angie found herself craving a man who wasn't good for her, and oh yeah, someone was out there trying to scare her, things were perfect.

She was, after all, alive, right? *Right*. In light of that, she impulsively ate pastrami instead of lean turkey for lunch. She had high-fat barbecue potato chips to go with it.

And then she drove to the library to see if the latest mystery had come in.

Lie. She wanted to see the woman who'd deserted her son. Sam's mother.

Behind the reference desk sat a woman nose deep in a stack of books. She had long, dark hair streaked with gray, which was pulled back by clips that didn't stop it from falling over her shoulder.

As Angie came closer, the woman looked up with sharp, light brown eyes and an easy smile.

Both stopped Angie in her tracks. She knew those eyes, that smile. "You're Sam's mother."

The woman opened her mouth, then slowly closed it again. Her expression went from helpful to unwelcoming in two seconds flat. "Who are you?"

"Angie Rivers. You…he looks like you."

Her mouth tightened. "Sam is young and ridiculously handsome. We look nothing alike."

Angie sat in the chair in front of the desk. "Oh, but you're wrong. I knew right away. It's in the eyes. There's no mistaking it."

"I…see." Sam's mother set down her pencil. "What do you want?"

There was no way to ease into this conversation. "I guess I want to know why you don't talk to him. Why you don't call him."

She frowned, her knuckles white on a book. Then she turned away.

"I'm sorry," Angie said to her ramrod-stiff spine. "I shouldn't have asked. He thinks of you, is all."

She didn't turn back. "Is he…all right?"

"Yes." Angie hesitated, then decided to go for broke. "He told me about you. About you not wanting to see him, since he's a cop like his dad."

"If he told you that, the two of you must be close." The woman's hands trembled. "Oh dear," she breathed, then covered her eyes before turning around again. "I think of him, too."

"He'd probably like to hear that."

"It's been so long. Are you his girlfriend?"

"Not exactly." Angie managed a weak smile. "He, uh, has a few issues in that area."

"Yeah." She reached for a stack of books and made herself busy separating them. "I'm sorry, I'm working."

Angie nodded and, taking her cue, walked away. Halfway across the room, she hesitated, then glanced back.

Sam's mother stood staring out the window, work forgotten, lost in thought.

But there was an achingly sad smile on her lips.

To avoid going home after work, Angie went to the bookstore to waste the hours before class.

Ellie Wilson was behind the counter, frowning as she added up something on her calculator. "Studying?"

"Always. How's business?"

"It'd be a heck of a lot better if people would just do their jobs."

"Employee trouble, huh?" Angie smiled sympathetically. "You haven't by any chance seen that guy I asked you about?"

Ellie's frown deepened. "For your cop?"

"Yes."

"You should stay out of that nasty business before something terrible happens."

Angie thought about the prank calls, the break-in, and nearly said, *Too late*. "I'll be okay."

"Well, just be careful." Ellie sighed and set aside her paperwork. "And no, I haven't seen him. Got enough to worry about. I never thought it would be this complicated and stressful to run a business."

"Is there anything I can do to help?"

"That's so sweet." This from George, who came out of the office. He gently set aside his wife and sent Angie a warm smile. "You're looking quite happy today. It's nice to see you that way after all you've been through."

"Thank you."

"You must have something special going on to be glowing like that." Ellie peered at her from over her spectacles. "You pining over that cop or something?"

"Uh…no." Not much anyway.

Okay, yes. Yes, she was, but she didn't have to admit it.

"Cops are terrible lovers," Ellie said with a shake of her finger. "Remember that."

Angie choked on a laugh. "That's quite a blanket statement."

"They're too sidetracked with their work," Ellie insisted, slapping George's hands away when he tried to steer her aside again.

Angie didn't know about all the other cops in the world, but given how Sam had kissed and touched her—as if she was the only woman on the entire planet—she had to say, Ellie was pretty far off base.

"Just watch out," the older woman warned, still pushing her husband aside. "Will you stop?" she said to him. "Men are traitors, Angie. Every one of them."

"Hey, not all," George corrected mildly.

Ellie rolled her eyes, and when George turned his back, Ellie mouthed, *All of them.*

* * *

After class that night, Angie walked to her car with a group of other students and purposely didn't allow herself to think about going home.

Alone.

Instead she concentrated on how lovely her day had been, doing as she pleased, filling her mind with new and exciting things.

It was late when she pulled into the carport of her apartment. For a moment, she sat in her car, staring at her apartment, wishing she'd had the insight to have left on lights.

Her cell phone sat in her purse.

Call if you need me, Sam had written.

Angie put her chin in the air. She was a big girl. Strong. Independent.

And only a little scared. So she got out of the car, walked up the path and…nearly had a seizure when Sam stepped out of the shadows and said her name.

"Holy smokes," she whispered, hand to her heart, which had skipped a beat at the tall, leanly muscled, grim-looking man waiting for her. "Don't do that! You scared the life out of me."

"I could say the same for you."

She had time to think he looked pretty darn amazing with that deep scowl on his tough face, when he held up his flashlight, illuminating a note that had been left taped to her door.

Mind your own business or die.

Chapter 9

"Pack a bag," Sam muttered. "You're coming with me."

Angie stopped in mid-pace of her living room and stared at him. They'd called the police, who'd already come and gone. "The police officer said they'd put a car on the street tonight."

Sam had waited with what he thought was admirable patience while Angie got the same old spiel from the cop that he'd himself given a million times.

Don't answer your door, ma'am.

Keep track of incoming calls, ma'am.

Call if whoever it is comes back, ma'am.

In other words, hang tight until she got hurt, or worse, in which case the cops would be able to do something for her.

"I don't care what they said," Sam said through his teeth, barely resisting the urge to haul her close and kiss all this stuff away, until it was just her and him, skin to skin, the rest of the world be damned.

But that would be beyond stupid, and Sam was anything but stupid. If he so much as touched her, all good intentions to keep his hands to himself would go right out the window. "Like I said, you're coming with me."

"Where?"

"My house."

Angie crossed her arms. "You don't look thrilled about the idea."

He decided not to respond to that. "Tell me you didn't chase any more suspects down an alley today."

"So you really think this is your guy?"

"I think it's a good possibility, unless you're tormenting some other criminals I don't know about."

Her mouth tightened, and he was afraid he recognized the look. Pure stubbornness. To avoid looking at her, he took out his cell and called Luke.

"Talk," Luke growled when he answered, sounding gruff and…busy.

"On a date?"

"So to speak."

"Did you track down John's roommate this evening?"

"Uh…" In the background, Sam heard a woman's low, sexy murmur.

"Bad timing, huh?"

"You could say so. But the roommate has, curiously enough, not come back as promised."

"Well, just to make it interesting, we've got another development. A note on Angie's door."

"Saying?"

"Back off or die."

"Hmm. Not so lightweight anymore, is it?"

"No." Sam's gut clenched. "I'll see you in the morning." He clicked the phone shut.

"I haven't seen the suspect in a few days," Angie said behind him. "I don't know why he'd bother with me."

"Because you seem to be the only one who can point him out."

"I'm staying here tonight, Sam."

Sam pocketed his phone and faced her. "I'm not leaving you alone. Don't ask me to."

"I'm not asking, I'm telling."

He stared her down, and after a long moment, she let out a long sigh. "You know, I really want to tell you to go to hell."

"Tell me whatever you want. I'm still not leaving you alone."

"I don't follow demands or take orders from anyone, Sam. But…"

"But…?"

She turned away. "Fine. I don't want to be alone either, okay? I don't want to be alone bad enough that I'll go with you. Just do me a favor and stay out of my way while I get my bag."

Angie came back into her living room a few moments later with a backpack on her shoulder. She stopped a breath away from Sam and tipped her head back to look at him. "I packed."

"Okay."

"And while I did, I did some thinking."

Uh-oh. "Okay."

A hint of a smile crossed her lips as she dropped her backpack to the floor and put her hands on her hips. Though she barely came to his chin, she managed to look down her nose at him. "You're furious, tense and worried. And now, you're surprised," she added. "Did you really think I can't see what's going on in your head by now?"

"Not many can," he muttered.

"Well, that alone should tell you something. But because you *are* furious, tense and worried, it tells me you care about me. Enough to want me with you."

"I want you safe."

"If that was the case, you'd send me to a friend's. To my parents. But you want me with you. Why can't you just say it?"

"Are you always this bossy?"

"No, as a matter of fact, it's a new thing for me." She smiled now, and it was a stunner. "And I like it. You know what else? I like you. I'm not sure why, but I like you. Okay, we can go now."

He took her pack, shouldered it. As she moved ahead of him, he found his hand at the small of her back. Not for her, but for him, because damn if he didn't want his hand on her.

At the touch, Angie craned her neck and smiled. One of those just-for-him smiles that did something ridiculous to his stomach.

With a scowl, he dropped his hand.

She simply reached for it, held it in her own. "I'm glad you're here," she whispered as they went out her front door.

She was glad. Great. She was glad and he felt like he'd been tied in knots, and every time she looked at him, smiled at him, the strings tightened inside, drawing him further in, making him care all the more. All professional detachment was gone, and he knew it. No amount of not touching, no amount of being as gruff as possible was going to change anything.

Outside he told the cop in his squad car that he was taking Angie, but to watch the house.

"You should know," he said to Angie, "you're done risking your pretty neck." He opened his passenger door for her.

"What?"

He stopped, framing her in between the truck door and his body, and though not a single inch of him touched her in any way, his entire frame quivered with awareness. "You're done going to night classes alone. Done coming home alone. Done trying to solve my case. Done with everything until this is over. Do you understand?"

She let out a little laugh, but when he didn't smile, hers faded. "You're not kidding."

"Nope." He shut the door, knowing he sounded like an ass but still so worked up and scared to death he didn't care. He walked around and slid in behind the wheel, feeling the weight of her stare. Sighing, preparing to be blasted by her anger, he looked over. "What?"

"You think my neck is pretty."

That was so far from what he expected her to say, he could only stare at her.

"And there's something else." She reached over to put her hand on his. "About me not doing stuff... you're talking from fear. I get that. I really do. But I can't give in here, Sam. I just can't. All I've ever wanted is a chance to fly. To be encouraged, to be loved for who and what I am."

His stomach landed on his feet with all this... mushy talk. "This isn't about anything other than your safety."

"It's about us."

She was right. God, she was right.

"Can you do it, Sam? Can you take me seriously that way?"

"What does that have to do with keeping you out of trouble?" he asked a bit desperately.

"I think you know what's going to happen if we're not careful. Alone together in your house."

"We're not a couple of horny kids."

"No, we're not. You're a passionate man. Intelligent, too. And incredibly sexy, Sam. Probably the most sexy man I've ever seen."

"You're not helping here, Angie."

"I'm about to. Because not even for you can I go back to my simple, complacent life." Her voice was terribly quiet, and drove right through his heart. "I agreed to your protection tonight, but—"

"No buts."

"But," she continued patiently, "I won't curb my new appetite for life. I hope you understand, I really do."

"It's just one night," he said desperately.

She looked directly at him, his greatest nightmare, his greatest fantasy, all wrapped in one beautiful package. "It's more," she insisted.

Sam's heart pretty much skipped a beat. "We're not sleeping together."

"Because *you're* scared."

"Because *you* can't separate love and sex."

"Can you?"

Her cell phone rang then, startling them both. She went to answer it, but Sam grabbed her wrist, turned it, so he could look at the readout.

"My mom," she told him.

Sagging back, he gestured for her to go ahead. While she talked, he drove. And tried not to think.

He might as well try not to breathe. His brain whirled. She wanted him. She was going to be sleeping at his house. He wanted her.

Ah, hell. Not good.

"Yes, school is great," Angie said into the phone,

then let out a slow, pent-up breath. "No, Mom, I'm still not going to medical school...not to law school, either. We've been through all this. This is for me— Yes. Yes, I know Tony said he could get me work at the district attorney's office, but that was a long time ago and I don't want to work there, I want— Mom." She sighed. "*Mom*—oops, hear that? Bad connection, gotta go. Love you, bye."

She tossed the phone into her purse, leaned her head back and closed her eyes.

Sam divided his gaze between the road and her face. She looked tired. Alone. And in spite of himself, he ached for her.

He waited until he'd parked outside his condo complex and turned off the engine. The street was deserted. The windows around them had started to fog, reducing his world to just the two of them. "Angie..."

"Let me guess," she said with her eyes still closed. "One of us is still sleeping on the couch."

"It's for the best." *Liar, liar.* "You should know, Angie...I don't do love."

Now she opened her eyes and looked at him. "Why not?"

"Because...I just don't."

"Because you're a big, bad, tough cop?"

"Partly because I'm a cop, yes."

"Oh, Sam." She shook his head. "What you do for a living doesn't matter to me as long as it makes you happy."

"Being a cop is who I am." The leather seats crinkled beneath him when he shifted subtly away from her. "It defines me."

"Yes, it does. So, what's the problem?"

"The problem is that you say it's fine now, but it won't be for long." Where had that come from? What was he saying? That if it wasn't for his job, he'd want her in his life? He'd actually give them a shot? God, he must be losing it.

"Sam…" She leaned forward and cupped his face in her hands. "You've lost your faith in love, that's all. You can get it back."

"It's not that. My job…not many understand it."

"I understand. I always would."

"That's a promise I doubt you could keep."

"Then you don't know me very well."

Her fingers, her cool fingers, skimmed over his face while her eyes gave him nothing but an earnestness that made his throat burn. "How could you promise such a thing?" he demanded. "Not even my ex-wife could."

Her eyes widened. "You…were married?"

"For all of six months."

"That's not very long."

"Long enough for Kim to realize being married to a cop was everything my mother had told her it would be. Namely bad."

Unable to stand the compassion in her eyes, her hands, he pulled back. He turned his head and looked out the window. "I don't expect any woman to be able to handle this life of mine."

"Yes, I can see you're quite attached to that idea."

He closed his eyes. "Look, I don't know how we got into this. Let's just get your bag and go inside."

She put her hand on his back. Lightly ran it over his tense muscles. He remained still, perfectly still, because if he turned and looked into her gaze, he might give in to this need for her that had him shaking like a damn newborn baby.

"Not all woman are like your mother," she said softly. "Or your ex. Some of us are far wiser."

He said nothing, just absorbed her amazing touch and tried to figure out why he liked it so much.

"In fact, some of us are wise enough to know when something is such an elemental part of you that it can't be separated out. *Shouldn't* be separated out." Her fingers slid up to the bare skin at the base of his neck. "You're a man," she whispered. "You're a cop. It's pieces of the pie, and you know what? I like all of it, every little piece."

"Angie—"

"I do," she said firmly. "I guess what I'm saying is…maybe someday you'll consider risking your heart one more time."

"Angie—"

"I know what I'm asking. I'm asking you to open up to all the hurt you promised yourself you'd never feel again, but Sam…life has to be lived."

"I live fine."

"Sam."

She waited until he looked at her, waited until he could do nothing but see her, really see her, and ache with all the yearning he didn't want to acknowledge. "I want a lot of things," she said. "I want this new life. I want to enjoy it. And I want you."

"Angie—"

"I would never turn away from you." Her fingers stroked his jaw. "Never."

He stared at her, and in complete earnestness, she held his gaze, never even blinking.

God. What would it take to believe? To just lean in and let her kiss away all his fears? He almost did exactly that.

She kept looking into his eyes, her own shining.

"I could keep telling you all this, over and over, if that would help."

"Don't."

She simply put her mouth to his.

Chapter 10

It was dark outside, darker yet in the truck, and still Angie felt a burst of light at the touch of her mouth to Sam's. It felt good, it felt right...until he stopped.

He looked at her so miserably her heart melted. "It was just a simple kiss," she said.

"It wasn't just a damn simple kiss. Nothing with you is simple."

A car drove by, briefly illuminating the grim lines of his face. Pride flared, and she slowly pulled back. "I see."

"Angie...I just want you safe."

"Yeah. You've said." She turned away, and when

he reached for her, she shrugged him off. "Okay, let's try this. First, please stop acting so concerned when it comes to me."

"What?"

"Because you're confusing the hell out of me. I think it was the way you kissed me."

"Oh, no. Wait a minute. You kissed me."

"I know." She covered her eyes. "And stop calling me, okay? Stop every damn thing when it comes to me, and then, maybe then, I'll be able to get my head back together." She reached for her backpack, thinking she would get out and walk home.

"Angie—"

"No. You don't want to talk, you don't want to think, you sure as hell don't want to feel. I don't know why I thought…oh, never mind." More angry at herself than him, she tried to open the door but it was locked, and then he was reaching for her, blocking her way.

"I shouldn't have come," she said stiffly, not facing him, trying not to feel the big, strong hands holding her in. "I should never have gotten involved with you."

"Damn right you shouldn't, but you did." He swore, then whipped her around to face him, no easy feat in the cab of his truck. "You did, and you're here, and damn you, even if you weren't I'd be thinking about you."

"Sam—"

"Oh no, don't shut me up now, I'm on a roll. You want me to talk? To think? To feel? I do all those things, for you. Only for you, Angie. I can't seem to stop." In the next breath, his mouth covered hers.

She tried to resist, honest to God, she tried, but he nibbled, coaxed, cajoled and finally ate at her resolve with such hungry, sexy bites she gave in with a small cry of surrender.

His hands urged her closer, over him, and with shocking ease, she straddled him right there on the bench seat of his truck. The kisses went on, hotter, deeper, wetter with each passing moment, punctuated by sighs and moans of pleasure as their hands got into the action, fighting for space.

Angie's anger vanished as heat and intense need surged through her body. He tasted good, so very good, and she was desperately hungry for him, the hunger fueled by the knowledge he felt the same about her whether he wanted to or not.

His mouth was greedy, and so were his hands. She held her breath as his fingers danced down the material of her sundress to the hem, then slowly returned, bunching up the dress as he went, using both hands now, on her bare thighs, scooting her even closer so that the very center of her slid over the vee of his jeans, and a most interesting bulge.

When she arched her hips, he let out a rough groan and filled his hands with her breasts. Humming with pleasure, she put her hands over his. "Sam, I need—"

"I know. Me, too." He unbuttoned the bodice of her dress, unhooked her bra, and spilled her breasts into his waiting hands. Leaning forward, he used his mouth, his tongue, his teeth until she was nothing but a string of taut nerves, quivering and edgy.

She had to touch him. Her hands slid through his hair, over his shoulders, his back, beneath his T-shirt to the sleek, bare, heated skin she'd been dying to feel. "More, Sam."

"More," he agreed, reaching around her to open the glove compartment, shoving maps and CDs to the floor, searching… *"Yes,"* he breathed, and held up a condom, which she took in her fingers.

His hands were back on her bare thighs, beneath her dress now, cupping her bottom, rubbing her over his most impressive erection, and all she could do was whisper his name, begging for more. In tune to the squeaking leather beneath them and the moans and sighs of their own breath fogging up his windows, he gave it.

He slid aside her panties and used his fingers to

bring her to a shuddering orgasm that hit her so fast she scared herself. When he opened his jeans, she caught her breath, stared down at him in wonder, and then taking the condom from his fingers, putting it on him herself, she impaled herself on him.

Filled to the limit, she let out a long, shuddering sigh that mingled with his quiet "oh yeah." Then he cupped her face, brought her down for another soul-destroying kiss as he began to move.

She wanted to come again, her entire body strained and writhed for it, and she couldn't believe it. She couldn't control her breathing, or the arching of her hips or the soft panting echoing in her ears. "Sam…"

"I know." He caressed her belly before gliding his hands to her thighs, holding them open for his thrusts while his thumbs brushed over the core of her. She sobbed out his name. He said hers, too, in a hoarse, tight whisper before he raised his hips and thrust so high inside her she exploded on the spot. Vaguely she heard the rough groan that told her he had found his release, too, in an explosion that shook his entire body.

Gasping, she set her forehead to his, wrapping her arms tightly around his neck, hanging on through the little aftershocks that rippled through her system, determined to stay this way forever. Darkness reigned, and all the windows had long ago fogged, so there was no outside, nothing but the two of them, alone, together. "Mmm." She sighed.

"Yeah." He waited until she lifted her face from where she'd plastered it to his neck. "I want you again," he said. "Inside this time. In my bed."

"Oh, yes."

He helped her right her clothing; slowly drew her bra closed, carefully tucking a nipple back in place, running a finger over the tip as he did, eliciting a shiver.

He looked up at her, eyes aglow. "You like that." To prove his point, he dipped his head and dragged his tongue over the hardened, aching point. "I want to taste the rest of you."

All she could do was nod.

He slid a finger down the bunched elastic of her panties, straightening them, the pad of his thumb stroking the very center of her being as he did.

She let out a horribly needy whimper.

His eyes darkened. His thumb stroked again, and again she made the sound.

"Inside," came his hoarse whisper. "Now." He skimmed the material of her dress down her legs while she quivered with the knowledge he'd nearly driven her to another orgasm while just dressing her.

"Inside," she agreed, and staggered against him when they got out.

He simply swept her into his arms, making her heart sigh. She was strong. Independent. But for right now, this was where she wanted to be, against him, with his arms tight around her.

Then the front door whipped open, startling them.

Luke took one good long look at both of them and grinned widely. "Well, look who the cat dragged in."

Angie, drugged in sensuality only a moment before, froze, her gaze on Sam's above her. The two of them were obviously glowing. How would he react to someone seeing them like this?

Embarrassed?

Angry?

Would he push her away?

Luke leaned against the doorjamb and continued to grin.

Sam scowled but didn't let Angie down. "Excuse me."

"Certainly." Luke shifted aside, and when Sam would have kicked the door closed on him, he neatly stepped inside first.

"I meant for you to be on the other side of it when it closed," Sam told him. "What happened to your date?"

"Didn't work out."

From the living room came the sounds of a ball game and the unmistakable scent of pizza. "I'm guessing you don't want to watch the game."

Angie tried to get down, but Sam held firm. "No." He looked slightly abashed but not ashamed, and definitely more than a little protective as he turned away so Luke could no longer see her.

At the endearing gesture, such a small thing really, but that he would think of it...her heart took a stumble.

But with her new angle of vision she could see into a mirror that hung above a small desk in the foyer. Sam stood there, towering and sexy. In his arms was this wild, mussed, erotic-looking woman—*herself.* Her mouth was still wet, her hair beyond rioted, and now that she could see up close and personal, she realized her buttons hadn't been fastened in the correct order and that her right breast was in danger of presenting itself. With a little squeak, she lifted her hands to fix the problem.

Sam didn't look much more together. His hair was standing on end—from her fingers—and his eyes blazed with the heat they'd just shared.

In the mirror, their gazes met for one long heart-beat, during which Angie's pulse started to race again.

They weren't finished. Oh, thank God, they weren't finished.

"Sorry," Sam said to Luke, still staring at Angie's reflection, then he started down the hall with her.

They were halfway to the bedroom before Luke called out. "I'll just leave the pizza and pick up something else for myself, since no doubt you're about to work up an appetite."

Sam just slammed his bedroom door, set Angie down on his huge, rumpled, unmade bed and followed her down.

He surrounded her with his arms, his body, the look in his eyes. "I've already worked up the appetite," he said, and bent his head to her body to prove it.

The sun speared through the bedroom window and rudely woke Sam up. He might have grumbled and growled and shoved a pillow over his head, only there was a weight on his pillow.

And on his body, too, he realized. Both his arms were numb and there was something sprawled over his body—

Angie.

He hadn't forgotten, but it'd been so long since he'd let a woman stay all night—

Wait. He'd never let a woman stay all night except his ex. And certainly not like this, all entwined like a pretzel, with no feeling left in any of his limbs.

His ex hadn't liked sleeping like that. She'd claimed he made her all hot and sticky. Couldn't have that, apparently. She'd slept all curled in a ball on her side of the bed, and woe was him if he'd attempted to invade her space.

There was some serious space invading going on here.

He was on his side, the numbest arm beneath Angie, the other over her hip. He had a handful of her very sexy butt, holding her close to him as if he never planned on letting her go. He had one leg thrust high between her thighs, and even now he could feel the heat of her.

She faced him, his little bed hog, completely relaxed in exhausted slumber since they'd finally fallen asleep only—he squinted at the clock—two hours ago. She had her nose pressed to his collarbone, one arm thrown over his neck and a leg tossed over his hip. Her breasts, bare and glorious and… damn it.

Her other hand was open on his chest, right over

his heart. He drew in a long, deep breath and braced for the panic.

Angie opened her eyes. Slowly. Easily. No grogginess for this woman, as her dark gaze landed right on him. "Morning," she said, her voice husky from sleep. Her hair tickled his nose, her body slid sensuously along his, making him want to purr in pleasure.

Then she smiled. A stunner. His heart actually stopped, because in that gaze wasn't simply lust. No, nothing as simple as lust. There were all sorts of terrifying things: arousal, relief, joy, affection.

And love.

He couldn't miss it. It was blaring at him, waiting for him to acknowledge it.

But he didn't believe in a happy-ever-after. He didn't believe in love. And wasn't sure he ever would. "Angie—"

She blinked, and the emotions that had so rocked his world vanished in that one flash of time, replaced by...

Nothing.

She pulled back from him, slid out of the bed and bent for her clothes. "Look at the time." She turned to him, covering her lovely body by holding her dress in front of it. "Can I use your bathroom?" she asked politely.

"Of course, but—damn it," he said to no one when she disappeared into his bathroom. He got out of bed, swore again when his numb legs quivered like a newborn baby, and went to the bathroom door.

Locked.

He knocked. "Angie?"

For an answer, the shower came on.

"Angie...open up." Nothing. "I guess you figured out I'm lousy at morning afters."

He imagined her soaping up, which did little for his very insistent morning hard-on. "Angie?" He knocked again. "I'm sorry, okay? Now let me in."

Steam began to come from under the door. He figured she was running her hands over her entire body now.

Which should have been *his* pleasure this morning, thank you very much. But he was too stupid to have finagled that, wasn't he. He put his forehead to the wood. "Look, I just had a moment of panic when I woke up and there you were, and—" And given the silence he wasn't doing this right.

The water turned off.

The door opened. She stood there wearing nothing but his towel wrapped around her delectable body. Lush, wet curves plumped out of the top of the towel while her tanned, toned thighs showed out the bottom. The towel was a tad too big for him to see anything else.

She put her hand to his chin and lifted his gaze so it met hers. "Is your moment of panic gone now?"

He opened his mouth, but he'd never lied in his life and he sure as hell wasn't about to start now.

"I see," she said quietly, and walked past him. Halfway to the bed, she dropped the towel.

His tongue nearly fell out of his mouth as she bent for her panties. "It's…somewhat gone," he managed to croak out.

"Somewhat isn't good enough." She stepped into her dress and pulled it up the length of her body, then started on the long row of buttons.

"I know a way that would greatly help," he said, and when she turned to look him over, he realized he was standing there bare-ass naked.

She cocked her head and, while she smiled, it didn't quite reach her eyes. "Tempting, but…" She lifted a shoulder. "I don't intend to push myself on you. Will you take me to work, please?"

Push herself on him? Hell, he was willing to beg. "Work isn't a good idea, not until we get a hold of this guy."

She tossed back her wet hair and put her hands on her hips. "What are you going to do, take me around with you all day long?"

Terrifying how tempting that sounded. "No, but you don't have to go out in public and be a target. We're going to get him, probably today."

"You're that close?"

"We're that close."

"I'm going to work, Sam. I'll be fine there." She slipped into her sandals. Used the towel that had been covering her body to dry her hair. Pulled up the blankets they'd tossed aside in their heated passion.

All without looking at him. He looked at her though, plenty. She smelled like his soap, *his* shampoo. And though she was entirely covered, he ached for her to be warm and naked and plastered against him, as she had been all night long.

But she was upset, and it didn't take a rocket scientist to know that was his fault. So he shoved his legs into his discarded jeans, wincing as he fastened them over his erection, and went to her.

"I've got to go," she said, resisting, but he turned her to face him.

"You're angry."

"Frustrated." She finally looked at him, her eyes filled with something that made him swallow hard. "And I just realized I'm never going to reach you, not the way I want to."

Regret was a two-fisted punch. "Angie—"

"Yeah, I know. Take me to work, Sam. I think we both need the space."

Space was exactly what he needed. Actually, he had no idea what he needed anymore.

Sam pulled up in front of the café and turned to Angie, looking like he needed coffee in the worst way.

Angie released her seat belt, reached for the door handle, then sighed and sat back.

She couldn't leave like this. He was miserable. She was miserable. All that misery radiated throughout the truck.

Worse, it wasn't his fault. He'd given her everything he could. She knew that.

She just wanted more.

Not fair to him, not fair at all. She'd known the rules when she'd made love with him. She'd gone into it with her eyes wide open.

And she would not hurt him simply because he couldn't be what she wanted.

"Promise you'll wait for me to pick you up after your shift," he said. "That you won't even think about going back to your apartment without me."

"Sam—"

"Promise me, Angie."

She stared up into his tense face. He hadn't taken

the time to shave, and the stubble on his jaw added to his edgy, dangerous expression. The black jeans and black T-shirt only lent credence to the fact.

But he didn't scare her. He never could. Nor could she resist him, it seemed. With another sigh, she leaned in and put her mouth to the bunched muscle on his jaw.

From deep in his throat came a low, rough sound. A helpless sound.

And her heart squeezed. Maybe he hadn't wanted to be touched by her, but he was. Whether he wanted to admit it or not, he was. "Angie, promise me."

She replaced her mouth with her hands, cupping his face as she pulled back far enough to meet his gaze. "I promise to let you be my hero."

"I mean it."

So tough. Trying to be so distant. But his eyes gave him away. "I mean it, too."

He stared at her for a long moment, as if assessing her for honesty.

She kissed him again, on the lips this time, very softly, very gently. "Have a good day."

He groaned and set his forehead to hers. "Damn it, I want to be mad at you. Don't ruin it for me."

She slid her arms around him and hugged him close. "I won't."

He groaned again, but his arms came around

her, too, warm and sure and strong. He slid his jaw against hers. "I want you to be safe. Do you understand that? God, you're really driving me crazy."

"I know." She sank her fingers into his hair and lifted her face to see his. "I don't mean to. I love you, Sam." Gently she put her fingers to his lips, before he could react. "I just wanted you to know." Kissing him one last time, she grabbed her purse and left the truck.

Chapter 11

Heart pounding, palms damp with sweat, Sam watched Angie walk away from him toward the café.

Say something to her.

Anything.

But he didn't, and she vanished inside without a glance back.

She loved him. Just like that. *She loved him.*

And she'd said it so...sweetly. So damn easily. So genuinely his heart clenched again, even tighter.

He nearly ran a red light. Twice. Cars honked at him. Lifting an apologetic hand and feeling like an idiot, he told himself to get a grip. He was a cop. He had important things to think about.

But nothing came to mind. Nothing at all.

Because nothing was more important than this, than her, and he knew it.

Angie smiled, laughed and talked during her shift, as always. But unlike always, her mind was elsewhere.

She kept picturing the mixture of panic and befuddlement on Sam's face as she'd left him that morning. Kept thinking about the reaction she'd hoped for, and hadn't gotten, to her proclamation.

Well, she should have known better. She *did* know better.

And yet oddly enough she didn't regret a thing.

After her shift, he was there waiting for her, just as promised. She'd expected no less. He got out of his car and opened the door for her. Got back in and drove.

All wordlessly.

She expected him to take her home. She expected him to get rid of her as soon as humanly possible.

She didn't expect him to drive up to a nice outdoor barbecue place, where they got a table with such ease she knew he'd made reservations ahead of time.

Which made this…premeditated.

The nerves kicked up a gear.

The live band played too loud for talking—probably not a bad thing. The music was good, and though there was much unspoken between them, Angie felt…happy.

They danced.

That he even knew how to do so startled her, but they found their own rhythm together. And when, during a slow number, he rubbed his jaw to hers while holding her in those amazing arms of his, her eyes welled.

"Don't," he whispered in her ear, his hands moving slowly up and down her back.

"No, it's okay." She managed a watery smile. "It's just that…I really like this."

"Yeah." He bent, put his lips to hers for a gentle, slow kiss. "Me, too."

He took her to his place after that, still quiet as he led her into his bedroom. To his bed.

She lifted her arms for him, but he didn't follow her down, not immediately. First he lit candles. Put on some soft music. Kicked off his shoes, moved close and pulled off his shirt.

He was beautiful, and in spite of everything, she ached for him. Then slowly, so slowly she ached all the more, he slid off her clothes, taking care to kiss every inch of flesh he exposed, until she lay before him, open to his gaze, quivering and tight with need.

He kicked off the rest of his things and Angie could only sigh because Sam by candlelight was the most magnificent thing she'd ever seen. Hard and sleek, he was poised over her, the muscles in his arms quivering as he tried to hold back.

But she didn't want him to hold back. Not ever. So she arched up and slid her body to his. Chest to chest, thighs to thighs, and everywhere in between, until he let out a harsh groan.

Towering over her, he looked down, his eyes aglow with need and affection and hunger…and the same bafflement that always broke her heart.

He still didn't know what to do with her.

But she knew what to do with him. "Love me," she whispered, pulling him down to her, opening her legs to make room for his body, loving how he felt between her thighs, all hard and throbbing. For her.

Still, he tried to hold back. "Angie—"

"With your body, Sam. That's all. Just love me."

Closing his eyes on a groan, he blindly searched out her mouth and did just that.

Loved her until the first hint of dawn.

* * *

The next morning, Sam masked his panic well, but Angie still felt it and, this time, ignored it. After his telling her they hoped to close in on the case by that night at the latest, she walked into the café alone.

Her boss was chopping up a red pepper, singing at the top of her lungs to her favorite country station and keeping an eye on the boiling pot on the stove.

"Whew, it's a chilly one." Angie hugged herself and moved closer to the stove, wondering if she would ever feel as warm as she had in Sam's arms. Wondering if she would ever get the chance to feel them around her again.

Josephine turned down the radio and gave her a long once-over. "What's the matter?"

"Oh…nothing." Angie put on her apron and tried to believe it.

"And nothing, I suppose, is why your chin is dragging on the ground." Josephine stirred the pot, which emitted a delicious scent. "You didn't get attacked in a bank again."

"No."

"Your apartment?"

"I wasn't there last night."

"Ah." Josephine stirred some more. "You were with your wow cop."

Angie looked out the window into the bright sun spearing through the fog and sighed. "He's not my cop."

"You make love last night?"

A little laugh escaped Angie. "That's a bit personal, don't you think?"

"Did you?"

"I'm not sure."

"Honey, if you're not sure, then I'm really worried about you."

"*I* made love," Angie said quietly. "I'm just not sure he did."

"Ah." Josephine stirred some more and nodded. "You think it was just sex for him."

Angie watched a couple walk down the street in the early-morning light, holding hands, laughing. Kissing. And said nothing because of the lump in her throat.

"Honey, you know, I don't like to push."

That got a laugh out of her. "Uh-huh."

"Oh, stop. Maybe I push, just a little." Josephine sniffed. "But I care about you."

"I know." Angie shoved away her melancholy and turned to smile. "I know. And I'll be fine."

"That man, he cares about you. Very much."

"He doesn't want to."

"He's afraid." When Angie looked at her in surprise, Josephine nodded. "Just because he's big and tough doesn't mean he can't fear. Matters of the heart terrify him. You need to be patient, that's all. And don't ever give up, not on something you want this much."

She did want him. With all her heart she wanted to believe it could happen, but there seemed to be so much stacked against them. "How do you know so much?"

"I'm ancient, that's how. Patience, Angie. You don't have a lot of that, but you need to try."

Angie laughed again, and oddly enough, felt a little better.

"Yes," said Josephine, slowly nodding, watching her. "This time around you're going to be just fine."

Sam spent the morning with Luke. No less than a dozen times he pulled out his cell phone and started to dial Angie.

And about a dozen times he swore colorfully and stuck the thing back in his pocket.

"You always talk dirty to your cell phone?" Luke asked.

"It's a new habit." This was asinine, this inability to do anything other than think of her. It had to stop.

But all he could think was, why hadn't he tried to tell her how much he cared about her?

He told himself they'd have plenty of time to talk later, and during that later, in which he planned on having her naked and beneath him, he'd try to tell her then.

If only he could figure out how to put it into words.

By break time, Angie decided Josephine was right. It was time to go for it, in all aspects of her life. One thing at a time, of course, and first up… her fears.

With her tips and check in her purse, she headed to the bank. Once there, she wasted a good five minutes on the sidewalk, staring at the building. She told herself she was sweating from the walk, from the sun. Not from fear.

I'm not afraid of anything anymore.

Anything but Sam not wanting her love, that is. But she'd done the best she could there, and looking back on it, how she'd fallen so unexpectedly for him, how she'd been open and honest with her feelings, she knew she couldn't have done anything differently. *Wouldn't* have done anything differently.

Life was to be lived.

With that, she lifted her chin and walked straight through the doors of the bank, straight toward the teller smiling at her, the teller who thankfully wasn't the same woman who couldn't open her drawer during the holdup.

Angie deposited her money without mishap and, with a relieved breath, walked back through the bank with a genuine smile on her face.

"Angie."

The sun was coming in the doors in such a way that the light sort of haloed the person in front of her. But she didn't need light to recognize Tony— tall, dark and handsome as ever in his expensive suit, chic sunglasses and smooth smile.

"Angie. You look—" he ran his gaze down her uniform and held there "—the same."

"Do I?" She grinned, because suddenly it seemed very funny. "I'm not."

"I've called you."

And she hadn't returned the calls. Petty, maybe, but it was her own little way of keeping the power. "I've been busy. I've gone back to school."

He removed his sunglasses. "I didn't know. That's fantastic. You'll be out of that dead-end waitressing job in no time." His eyes became warmer. "Why don't you call me when you're finished? I'll hook you up with a job in the district."

"I'm not going to be an attorney, Tony."

His eyes registered surprise. "You're…not?"

She kept smiling and shook her head. "I'm going to be an art history teacher with a serious painting hobby."

"A…teacher?" He cocked his head, considering, then nodded. "Well, that's good, too. I approve."

"Really?"

"Yes."

"That's nice. But I don't need your approval." Gently, because after all, at one time she had cared for this man, she set her fingers to his chin to close his mouth.

Then she waved and walked around him, out of the bank, and onward to the rest of her life.

Sam and Luke finally got a break when they located John's roommate…John Manning. They found him serving burritos to high-school kids on lunch break.

"Welcome to Burrito Palace," the short, chunky twenty-year-old said to Sam and Luke. "We have lots of specials going. What can I get for you today?"

Sam flashed him his badge. The punk paled and crossed himself.

"God isn't going to help you today, John," Luke said easily. "I'll take three tacos though, and—" He caught Sam's hard stare and sighed. "Never mind. Tell your boss you're taking a break. A long one."

They took him to the station, offered him a deal. They'd be lenient on him if he helped them. Turned out, the kid really was just a disgruntled friend, and not involved in the credit-theft ring. His father provided his college funds, plus he realized a life of crime wouldn't help his hopeful law career.

But he did recognize the picture of their suspect, who was apparently also a very *ex*-friend, and the son of the ringleaders. Tommy something or another. John gave them an address, and Luke and Sam got into Luke's car.

Following the directions John had given them for Tommy, Sam knew a deepening dread he couldn't explain. And it wouldn't go away.

"This feels very wrong," Luke said, suddenly and ominously echoing his worries.

"Yeah."

"I wish I knew why."

"Me too." Despite his best intentions to the contrary, Sam kept thinking of Angie. It was strange. He'd come to the conclusion he needed to try to tell her how he felt, so why couldn't he get over the feeling he'd be too late?

She loved him. *She* hadn't let her fears rule her. She'd just come right out and told him.

So why hadn't he told her?

Because he'd let his past color it. He'd told himself, over and over, no woman could or would ever love him as he was, and he'd come to believe it.

But he'd been wrong, and was still trying to get used to that.

They came to the end of John's directions. Both of them looked out the window at the typical Southern California suburbia in front of them. Ranch-style house, in a row of other similar ranch-style homes, all built in the 1970s. Nice yards, most with bikes in the driveway, or other various kid toys. SUVs and flowered yards abounded.

"Middle-town, U.S.A.," Luke said, watching a man mow the lawn. "Only things missing are the two-point-four kids playing in the yard."

"Yeah." Sam reached for his radio. "But hell if I can figure out what's bugging me." He radioed dispatch to run the place and then they got out of the car.

No one was home.

The man mowing the lawn turned out to be the

landlord, who, after looking over their badges let them in.

The kitchen was small, cozy and very clean. On the wall was a portrait of a smiling kid...their suspect.

"Tommy?" Luke asked.

"Apparently." Sam moved on down the hallway, past a few bedrooms that looked orderly and tidy, to a closed door.

"What are you looking for, something obvious like...?" Luke broke off with a long whistle. "Like that, I suppose."

The room was a gold mine, lined with shelves filled with bins of mail. All *stolen* mail, if myriad addresses and names on the obvious bills and statements meant anything.

Another dead giveaway was the state-of-the-art computer equipment along one wall, including special laminating tools of the trade for ID theft.

"Definitely hit the lottery," Luke agreed. "Now let's get out of here and get our search warrant and come back all legal-like, shall we?"

They were halfway back to the station when Luke looked at him casually and said, "You have lipstick on the corner of your mouth. Looks like a very pretty shade of berry."

Sam licked his lip and tasted Angie. "You might have told me that two hours ago."

Luke just grinned. "And ruin your illusion that I have no idea what's going on between you two?"

"You *don't* have any idea what's going on."

"No, *you* don't. Me, now I have a pretty good idea."

Before Sam could respond to that, his cell phone rang.

"Uh…Mr. O'Brien?" said a hesitant voice. "This is John Manning." The sounds of Burrito Palace came over the line. "Like, I remembered Tommy's last name. It's Wilson. Tommy Wilson."

At the same moment, dispatch radioed them with the information on the house they'd just been in.

The renters? Ellie and George Wilson.

Tommy's parents. But that was the least of their problems. Sam's head snapped up as it all clicked into place. "Ellie and George Wilson… *God*. They're the couple that runs the bookstore next to the café where Angie works."

Luke shook his head. "Does Angie know them?"

"She says they're friends—" He swore again, more viciously now. "Drive, Luke. Drive."

Luke had already hit the gas pedal. "Driving."

"Faster." He shoved his fingers through his hair.

"I can't believe it. Ellie and George are running the identity-theft ring."

"With Tommy."

"John's friend."

"*Ex*-friend," Luke added.

"Whom Angie kept seeing going in and out of the alley behind the bookstore."

"Yeah. I bet there's also an interesting room filled with interesting evidence at the bookstore."

"I'm also betting that Angie identifying John probably pissed his mommy and daddy off but good," Luke noted grimly. "Enough to make them start terrorizing her." He dialed Angie's cell phone.

"Think they're all talk?"

"With how much money they have at stake?" Sam shook his head. "No way." He swore again and leaned forward, as if that could get them there faster. *Pick up, pick up,* he silently urged Angie as her phone rang in his ear.

When she finally answered, he sagged in relief, flooded with so many emotions he could barely get his tongue wrapped around the words he needed. "Angie. Thank God."

"Sam?" Her voice changed, became a bit uncertain, and Sam cursed himself for that. She didn't know where they stood, and that was his fault.

They had plenty to talk about. Mostly *he* had plenty to talk about, but that would have to wait now. "The case," he managed, more unnerved than he could ever remember being. "We ID'd the kid."

"The suspect?"

"Yeah." They caught both a red light and traffic. Damn it. "Angie, I don't have time to tell you everything right now—"

"It's okay." Her voice was even enough, but he heard the hurt. "Goodbye, Sam."

"No, wait! You need to stay at work. Okay? Wait right there for me."

"I never wanted to be your responsibility."

"I know, but that's not what I meant. I'm almost there—"

"Look, Sam…" She lowered her voice to the soft whisper that always made his heart leap. "I didn't tell you I love you to hurt you, or make you feel obligated in any way."

"I know that, I—"

"I just wanted to share it, to tell you how I feel. That's all."

"Angie." He spoke through his teeth. "I'm on my way to get to you. Just stay right where you are. *Don't leave the café.*"

"But I already did."

He went very still. "What?"

"I went to the bank. I had to, really, but guess what? I made it without panicking. I even ran into Tony, which was nice because it was sort of a closure thing, and—"

"Angie." He closed his eyes, gripped the dash. "I want to hear all this. I swear, I do. Just later. *Where are you now?*"

"I'm on my break."

He tried to remain calm. "Where exactly are you on your break?"

"Just right next door…at the bookstore."

Chapter 12

Angie shifted her cell phone to her shoulder, cranked her neck to hold it in place, and attempted to balance the books she had spread in her lap so that she could hear Sam better.

She sat in the self-help section, trying to decide which part of her life needed the most help. She had *The Guide To A Complete Make-Over, How To Deal With Alpha Men* and *Using The Star Alignment To Your Favor* pulled out so far, and figured at best one of them applied to her.

Maybe all of them.

Then she'd heard Sam's voice and her stomach had dropped. He sounded so serious, so tense, and suddenly, in that one horrifying moment, she understood.

He was trying to tell her he couldn't see her again.

"Angie?"

"It's okay," she said, gripping the phone and trying to make it true. "I know what this is about."

"You do?"

"Yes, and listen…I understand." Well, not really, but she could try. "I'm fine."

"She's in the bookstore," she heard him say to Luke, who swore as colorfully as Sam had. "Baby, listen," he said to her now. "Get out of the store."

Baby. He'd called her baby. A man who was about to dump her, a man who sounded very intent, very focused…would he call her baby? "I'm studying."

"Drop everything and get out."

"But—"

"Where are you exactly?"

Angie looked at the aisle header that read Self-Improvement and decided that was just too pathetic. "Uh…in the nonfiction section."

"Alone?"

She looked around, puzzled. "Completely."

"Get the hell out. Don't hang up, I want to talk to you while you do it. Are you moving yet?"

Trusting him implicitly, even if he was going to break her heart, she set the books out of her lap. "Working on it."

"Okay, good. Keep moving, faster now. I'll be there in person in about seven minutes. Are you at the exit?"

Oh yes, he was intense. And very, very serious. But now she could hear the rest, could hear what else was in his voice, stopping her heart.

Pure fear.

She gripped the phone as she started out of the aisle. "Sam, what's the matter?"

"Just tell me you're out of the store, in the street in broad daylight with a throng of people around you."

"Not yet." His fear was contagious, and though she had no idea what he was dealing with, she kept moving. "Hold on a sec, I'm going to put you in my pocket so I can balance my stuff better." She slid the phone into the front pocket on her denim skirt, making it easier to balance her purse and the schoolbooks she'd intended to study before she'd been sidetracked by the self-help section.

Now all she had to do was get down the front stairs and outside. Then he'd feel better, and she could find out what was going on.

She came around the end of the aisle and plowed

right into… *"Ellie,"* she said in surprise. "I'm just—"

"Coming with me," the older woman said, and grabbed her wrist. "I have something to show you."

"You do?" Angie wondered which book had come in to make Ellie so eager. Her eyes were glowing and her cheeks flushed. She looked more excited than Angie had ever seen her.

But Sam had been adamant. She was to get out of the store. "Ellie, I have to go, I'm sorry."

"I don't think you understand. This way, please."

Because Angie was surprised at her adamance, Ellie managed to get her halfway down the next aisle and near the back office before she dug in her feet. "You're hurting my wrist."

"Well, that would make us closer to even then, my dear, because you're hurting me, too. In fact, you're killing me."

"I don't know what you mean."

"And I thought you were such an innocent."

The suddenly vicious tone from Ellie's mouth surprised Angie, so much so that she hesitated, which gave Ellie the advantage.

The older woman dug her nails into Angie's arm and jerked. When Angie opened her mouth, maybe to scream—she really had no idea—Ellie did something even more unexpected.

She pulled out a gun.

Angie stared at it, then lifted her head. "I don't understand."

"You will." Ellie moved behind her and shoved. Angie nearly fell forward but caught herself and started to turn around.

That's when Ellie shoved the gun into her spine. "Don't move," she said quite conversationally, "or I'll be forced to kill you. A shame that would be—I've just had these carpets done."

Angie swallowed hard against her rising fear. The barrel of the gun felt as if it were jabbing right through her flesh, but she knew it was nothing compared to what an actual bullet would do.

As it had in the bank holdup, Angie's sense of absurdity seemed to take over. She was wearing new panties today, thank God, though that was more in Sam's honor than anything else, as she'd had high plans for the evening ahead.

She'd watered her plants just that morning. And, oh yes, she'd gone to the bank. No checks would bounce.

Good, that was good.

But God, oh dear God, she wanted to live. She wanted to finish school. Paint. Teach.

Love Sam.

He was in her pocket, on the cell phone. Had he disconnected? No, he wouldn't, not when he'd so clearly wanted to hold on while she left the store—

He'd known. He'd known and had tried to get her out of here. What was it he'd said? He was only seven minutes away. That had been at least three minutes ago, hadn't it?

Ellie cocked the gun.

He'd be listening, horrified, helpless. A man like Sam would really hate to feel helpless. He'd blame himself.

Well, she just couldn't let anything happen, that was all. She'd find a way to keep Ellie talking until she could run free or somehow get control of the gun.

I love you, Sam. No matter what happens, I love you.

She wished she could take the phone out of her pocket and tell him directly, but she was afraid to do that, afraid to alert Ellie to the fact help was hopefully only moments away from charging in here.

And knowing Sam, he *would* charge in here. He'd put his own life on the line for hers. The thought made her throat tighten unbearably, and she moved very carefully, very purposely, telling herself she would do whatever it took to keep him safe. Alive.

"There are other customers in here," she said with what she thought was remarkable calm. "Ellie, someone is going to see you."

"Oh, no, they won't. I shooed out the only other customer I had when I overheard your phone conversation with your big, nosy cop. I knew it was time, even though I wasn't quite ready. You'll have to pay for that, too, as that other customer had a nice armful of books she never got the chance to pay for. You just keep racking up the debt to me."

Another hard jab of the gun to her back, and Angie bit her tongue rather than give Ellie the satisfaction of hearing her cry out.

"Keep walking," Ellie said sharply. "Behind the counter, that's a girl. Now into the office you go."

Angie put her hand on the door handle but hesitated, biting her lip through another malicious jab of the steel. "It's not too late, Ellie. Whatever you've done, it's not too late."

"You're right about that. Move along."

George was there behind a desk, head bent over some paperwork. When Angie walked in, he looked up and went pale as a ghost. "Ellie, no!"

"Oh, not you, too," Ellie said in disgust. She

propelled Angie into a chair. "It's done, so don't start."

George rose to his feet, looking shaky. "But taking a hostage? And our own little Angie? That was never discussed. I won't be a part of it."

"You already are, so sit back down and be quiet while I think a moment."

To Angie's dismay, George did as his wife said, just sat back down, looking as if a good wind would blow him over if he didn't.

Ellie started to pace. "Why couldn't you be scared off?" she demanded of Angie. "Anyone else would have gotten the message."

"So it was you?" It all seemed so far-fetched. Ridiculous. "In my apartment? Making those calls? The holdup at the bank?"

"Not the bank." Ellie made another lap around the office, being careful to keep the gun trained on Angie. "But that started the whole thing."

Had it been seven minutes yet? It certainly felt like it. It felt like a lifetime.

"It's where you met your cop. Decided to have a life-altering experience and solve his case."

"But what does that have to do with you?"

"That suspect you wanted so badly? He's the only employee who ever earns me any money."

She said this with a disgusted look toward George. "Tommy's my son."

On the outside, Ellie looked like the same woman as always, every hair in perfect place in its twist. Lipstick on. Sweater set without a wrinkle.

But her eyes were different, lit with a cruelty Angie had never noticed before. "Your son? Your son is a criminal?"

Ellie locked the gun on Angie so quickly her head spun.

"Now, Ellie, let's calm down," George interrupted. "She was just surprised—"

"Oh, shut up." Ellie narrowed her eyes. "Just shut up and let me think."

To Angie's disappointment George once again seemed to sink into himself and refused to look at her. Ellie continued her pacing. Each time the woman briefly turned away, Angie wondered if she had the courage to leap after her. She could do it. She still didn't believe Ellie would shoot anyone in cold blood, even if she appeared to have lost her marbles.

Ellie made another round.

Then another.

The next one, Angie promised herself. *I'll leap, tackle her down and wrestle the gun free.* Her heart started to pound, her every muscle quivered as Ellie paced toward her.

Come on, one more turn.

"You just couldn't give it up," Ellie said in disgust. "You had to keep pushing and pushing for information. You were bound and determined to get Tommy in trouble."

Two more steps and she'd make another turn.

"Pushing and pushing," Ellie kept muttering, and then she spun on her heel to begin another round of pacing.

Standing up, Angie took a flying leap.

George cried out, a warning to Ellie, an encouragement to Angie, she'd never know which. But at the sound, Ellie whipped around.

With Angie in midflight, Ellie aimed and fired.

The echo of the blast deafened. And everything switched to slow motion.

Angie's fall to the floor.

The unspeakable burning ripping through her.

She might have even cried out, but her ears weren't working any better than her motor reflexes. She hurt more than she could have imagined, and her hand slipped into her pocket as she fell, cupping the cell phone as if she could gain some comfort from Sam that way.

Could he still hear?

She hit the floor hard but didn't feel it. Maybe it was shock, but she lay where she landed, holding the phone, her lifeline, as an odd warmth came over her.

Then everything started to fade to black.

At the unmistakable sound of the gun going off, Sam's heart all but stopped.

"What is it?" Luke asked as he drove the crowded streets at a wincing speed.

"I think she's been shot." Sam strained to hear something from Angie.

And got nothing. Instead he heard George, who appeared to be ranting and raving at Ellie.

"Anything?" Luke demanded, simultaneously talking to dispatch.

Unable to speak, Sam shook his head. He didn't want to believe it, but his gut was always right.

Angie had been shot.

Luke let out a string of obscenities that would have impressed Sam at any other time, and finally screeched into the parking lot of the bookstore. "Let's go."

Sam stared down at his cell, horrified in a way he couldn't remember ever feeling before. If he'd lost her…my God. He couldn't even think it.

"Sam." This was accompanied by a hard shake, and Sam blinked Luke into focus.

"We're armed and we have backup on the way. Are you okay?"

"Yeah."

"No, you're not."

He was right. Sam had to be able to shift this aside. He had to focus if he was going to function in there as a cop.

"Sam."

"Yeah." He shook his head, blew out a hard breath and very purposely put the thought of Angie, bloody and lifeless, out of his head.

"Better," Luke said, eyes sharp. "Now. You ready? Really ready?"

A grim calm came over Sam and he checked his gun. "Ready."

Chapter 13

They entered the eerily silent store with guns drawn. "The office," Sam said to Luke. "That's where they took her."

Luke nodded, and they made their way through an aisle that had a handful of books on the floor of the otherwise incredibly neat store. Sam stared down at the books and knew that's where Angie had been. Right there, kneeling, innocently browsing. Fists clenched, he moved faster, behind the counter, toward the closed office door.

No sound came from behind it.

Expecting the worst, Sam and Luke charged into

the office, guns drawn. Sam was deadly calm. He was a cop.

Just a cop.

And this was a job, a job he knew well. He would do what it took, *whatever* it took, to insure the hostage's safety. Assuming she was still alive.

For a brief flash, his heart cracked, and the image of Angie came to him, sweet and loving and…dead. This he ruthlessly put aside. He couldn't function if he put her face to this nightmare, he just couldn't.

Then he saw her. She was sitting on the floor, her sweater covered in blood.

Next to her was Ellie, trussed with rope and a handkerchief stuffed in her mouth.

Above them both stood George, holding a gun on his struggling, furious wife.

At the sight of Sam and Luke standing in the doorway, guns trained on him, George went from disgruntled husband to cool criminal, and shifted his aim to Angie.

Her glasses had slipped off, and besides the fact she was squinting uselessly, she was also wildly bleeding. She had a hand over the spot and as Sam watched, she weaved as if she were going to topple over.

"Don't come any closer," George said amicably.

"She's shot," Sam said hoarsely. "Let me—"

"No."

But Sam started to move closer anyway, his mind only on Angie.

"Stay right where you are," George said very coolly. "Unless you want her to take another one." George nodded when Sam stopped short. "Yeah. Wise move."

Sam's gaze flickered over Angie. So much blood. And God, she was pale, so very pale. But her beautiful brown eyes were right on him, squinting with the lack of glasses, but definitely locked on him. Trusting.

Full of love.

His own burned. "Let's just let her out of here, okay? She can take an ambulance ride and we'll figure the rest out without her."

"Nope." George never shifted, never showed an ounce of nerves. "But I'll tell you what. If you stop moving toward me, she'll live. Don't underestimate me now, I mean it. You might think I look harmless, but believe me, I'm good and pissed—" he glared at his wife, who screamed in frustration from behind the handkerchief and stomped her trussed-up feet "—and just about ready to see how good my old aim is."

Sam noted George's hand didn't shake at all, and

figured his aim might be just fine. "Put the gun down."

"I don't think so." Slowly and purposely George cocked the gun, the noise echoing into the room.

Ellie continued to fight her bonds and make a terrible noise behind her restraints.

"Ellie, shut up or I'll shoot you next."

Ellie shut up.

"Good girl. You know, I'm really tired of this, damn tired. I should just shoot all of you and be done with it."

Sam kept his eyes on Angie. He'd give his own life to be able to scoop her close and hold on forever. He knew cops would be streaming all over the place in a matter of minutes. It wouldn't be long before Angie would be safe. "Talk to us," he said. "We know this is about the identity-theft ring. And your son."

"It is," George agreed. "How long have you known?"

"Not long enough to stop you."

"All I ever wanted was to have enough money to go live on a beach somewhere with a stack of good books," George said wistfully.

"So you started stealing other people's money."

"Stealing is rather harsh." George looked

insulted. "Let's call it borrowing. Used their credit a bit, it's really just a temporary thing."

Ellie started squirming again, and George shook his head. "Not for my wife though." He let out a long-suffering sigh. "She's greedy, folks, and I'm not ashamed to tell you, it's getting on my nerves. We started this whole thing simply to retire. And then she wanted more. Always more."

George looked at Angie and made a little grimace. "And you, you just couldn't let it go. You might think getting held up in that bank was the worst thing that ever happened to you, but in truth, it was the worst thing that ever happened to *me*."

Angie looked at Sam, gave him one of those just-for-him looks that had melted him from the very first day. And he gave it back to her, or tried. He had no idea if he was even close, as he'd never tried to tell a woman anything with only his eyes before.

Hers filled, so he figured he came close enough.

"You're worse than a bloody hound dog," George continued to Angie. "I never wanted you hurt though." He took in all the blood and winced. "I just wanted to stop paying my son to dig through people's trash for credit information. I wanted to be done falsifying and duplicating documents in order to charge against accounts that didn't belong to me. I had enough money, damn it, but she just wouldn't stop. Nag, nag, nag. She always wanted more." He sent another dark look to his wife. "I want to be done living with a shrew who harps on me for every little thing. I want that beach, the books…that's it. That's all. Happy ever after."

"You got more than that on your hands now," Sam assured him. "You've got a record. You're a criminal, and so is your wife and your kid. You're going to have to pay."

"I won't go to jail."

"Cooperating would be good," Luke suggested. "It would help. You can start by letting Angie out of here to get the medical attention she needs."

"How about you let *me* out of here. In exchange, Angie and Ellie."

Behind her bonds, Ellie growled and thrashed around, making George lift his hand to point out she'd proved his point. "See? She's a nightmare. *She's* the one who used the gun on Angie. Keep her and let me go. That's my deal. Take it or leave it."

And in that moment, Sam knew there wasn't going to be an easy out. George wasn't going to give up and surrender.

Luke looked at him and in his eyes, Sam saw the same knowledge. As always, they were on the same page. All they had to do was get George's gun off Angie long enough that Sam could take him down without risking more shots.

But then Angie's eyes fluttered, and with what looked like a huge effort, she blinked, trying to stay focused on him.

His sense of urgency, already screaming, increased a millionfold.

They were losing her right here, right now.

Angie wouldn't have agreed. Sure, there were spots dancing in front of her eyes. Large gray spots that made focusing a challenge, but she was all there.

The unbelievable searing pain in her body proved it. She didn't dare look down, as the sight of blood always made her weak. Just last week she'd given herself a paper cut deep enough to draw blood and, much to Josephine's disbelief, she'd actually had to sit down with her head between her knees.

Nope, she wasn't going to look.

But she hadn't imagined anything could hurt so bad. She almost preferred passing out, but if she did, she couldn't keep her eyes on Sam. And she did have her eyes on the man, terrified that he'd somehow get himself killed right in front of her.

He was looking at her, too, as if he wanted to both haul her close and yell at her for getting hurt.

That was her Sam.

Then she realized he was silently communicating something to her. He needed her help.

He needed her.

She found that a good feeling. Being needed by the strongest man she'd ever known. She could get used to that.

His eyes were still on her, calm and steady, and she nodded. He was going to let her have a hand in their fate. Trusting him implicitly, she waited, knowing they could do this. Together.

But she hoped he acted fast because her body felt as if it was on fire. She wasn't going to make it much longer. Struggling, she tried to get up.

"Stop," George said when she was on her knees, weaving wildly. "Don't move again."

A dizzy nauseousness rolled through her belly. "Not moving," she said. She couldn't move again, at least not without throwing up.

"I mean it," he said in a light voice that he might have used to chat over tea. "I'll shoot you in the thigh this time."

Angie believed him. But at least she was up on her knees now, not helpless, and wouldn't ever be again.

"George," Sam said, continuing to look into Angie's eyes with an expression that made her breath catch. "There's one thing you've forgotten."

"Of course there's not," he said, and for one flash took both his eyes and gun off Angie to glance at Sam.

Now, Sam's eyes told her, and with every ounce of courage she had, she tossed herself to the side and out of the way. Someone screamed, but then her hearing faded.

Except for the scream, that is, which annoyingly enough, went on and on and on, echoing in her head.

Sam took a flying leap at George. They landed hard, and rolled.

And rolled.

Then the gun went off. Angie knew this because her hearing came back for that one explosion, then vanished again.

Then men were spilling into the room from the door, from the window, and her vision was blocked.

Surreal time took over, just like at the bank. She was jostled when Ellie started to struggle anew, her face red with rage.

Angie thought maybe she cried out because she hurt so badly. *Sam. Where was Sam?*

A uniformed man knelt by her, and though his mouth was moving, she couldn't hear him.

Get out of my way, she wanted to say. *I can't see Sam.*

But the pain crept up on her now and she couldn't get rid of it, couldn't speak. Only a few moments before, with the adrenaline pumping through her body, she'd been able to forget the pain for a few seconds at a time. Not now. It clawed through her like nothing she'd ever experienced.

"Sam," she managed.

Someone, *several* someones, she thought fuzzily, urged her to lie down. One of them ripped the material at her shoulder, jarring her, and she cried out because, while she couldn't hear and could hardly see, she sure as hell could feel, and her entire body was on fire.

Why was that again?

"It's bad."

"Keep her still."

"I'm putting pressure on the wound."

"Lots of blood."

Then the men hunched over her were shoved aside, and Sam dropped to his knees with the most intense expression she'd ever seen on his face, and she'd seen plenty.

He was looking at her body, doing something, pressing in a way that made her stars dance faster, brighter. *"Angie."*

Oh, that voice, she thought dreamily, feeling herself smile. She would never get tired of that voice. She closed her eyes to hear it better.

"Angie. God."

She opened her eyes. "We did it, didn't we? We caught the bad guys."

"Yes. Oh, baby, I'm sorry." His voice was lower than normal, and full of agony as he gently scooped her close to him with his free hand, the other still pressing hard near her collarbone.

"Don't be sorry." She pressed her nose to his throat. A nice sort of numbness was taking over. "I'm tired now."

"No, don't close your eyes. Talk to me. Angie, talk to me." He hugged her tight and she sucked in a sharp breath as pain speared through her unexpectedly, reminding her fuzzy brain she had been hurt.

"Sam? Can you…call me baby again?"

"Baby," he said. "Now stay awake if you want to hear me say it again."

She smiled and drifted nicely on that for a while.

"Where's the damn ambulance?" Sam shouted above her in the scary-cop voice.

Wasn't that just like him. Hiding his fear with a shout. "I'm okay."

"Don't talk," he demanded, then proceeded to yell orders at everyone around them.

"I just can't believe it was Ellie and George." Knowing that hurt almost as much as her body did.

"I know." He pressed his mouth to her temple. "You were so damn brave, Angie."

He thought she was brave.

His mouth was bleeding and he had a cut over one eye. From his tussle with George, she realized. His shirt was ripped, and she thought maybe he'd never looked more...*hers*. "You're so pretty," she whispered.

He looked down at her, at something below her neck, and paled. "Angie."

"I want to marry you," she said dreamily, picturing it in her head. "And have a son just like you."

"Just be still," he begged, looking terrified. "Don't move."

She figured it was the marriage thing that made him so pale. "I scare you, I know."

"You're scaring the hell out of me," he agreed, his hands holding her still when she tried to sit up. "Now shut up. Can you do that while I try to get your bleeding under control?"

Oh, yeah. She'd been shot. She lifted her head, forced her eyes to focus and took a peek. "Oh… my." Her entire torso was awfully red. Bright red. Her stomach rolled. "Is that…blood?"

Then she passed out before she could hear the answer.

Chapter 14

Sam was already on his knees or he'd have fallen to them and prayed to a God he wasn't sure he believed in anymore.

Instead, he continued applying pressure to Angie's wound in spite of her moan of pain. "Don't move," he demanded, burying his face in her hair. "Hold on. You've just got to hold on."

Luke hunkered at their side. "The ambulance is nearly here, sweetie," he said to Angie. "Just take it easy for a moment, okay?"

She didn't respond and Sam nearly had a coronary. "Angie? Talk to me."

Nothing.

Bending closer, he rubbed his jaw to hers. "I love you, Angie. Please open your eyes."

Her eyes remained closed. Lifeless. "Damn it, where is that ambulance?" he shouted.

"Here." A medic appeared at his side, reached for her.

They started an IV and prepped a gurney while Sam sat there, gripping Angie's lifeless hand in his, unable to take his eyes off her.

"She'll make it," Luke said.

He nodded, because anything else was unacceptable. He could hardly bear to look at her. It used to be he could hardly look at her because she was so happy, so full of life, so joyous she hurt him just by being.

Now it killed him to look at her so still, so pale, but he forced himself as they loaded her up, forced himself to keep his eyes on her as they left the office.

On the sidewalk outside, Ellie and George were being loaded into separate police cars.

George hesitated, looking down at Angie with sorrow. "Sorry," he whispered.

"You got what you deserved," Ellie said, her eyes cold as ice.

"So will you," Sam promised.

For a moment, her detachment vanished. "You can't prove anything."

"We can prove everything," Sam told her before turning away to watch Angie being loaded into the ambulance. He started to climb in after her, only to be stopped by a medic who looked barely old enough to vote.

"Sorry, sir." The kid, a good eight inches shorter and nothing but a slim beanpole, swallowed hard. "You'll have to catch another ride."

"Move aside."

"Sir, you can't—"

"Bullsh—"

"I'll drive you," Luke said, hauling Sam back. "We'll get there just as fast, trust me."

Sam took one last glance at the closing doors on the ambulance and nodded.

The first time Angie opened her eyes, the overhead light hurt her eyes. Her body hurt, too; in fact, it felt as if a Mack truck had hit it. It was no problem at all to let sleep claim her again.

The next time she woke, the light had been turned to dim. Confused, she blinked and saw that the room around her was white.

She was in a hospital bed.

Slumped in a chair by her side was Sam, his arms

folded on the side of her bed at her hip, his head down, his shoulders rising and falling evenly with his slow, deep breathing.

She stared at him for a long, long time, the steady cadence of his breathing incredibly soothing, until the wooziness overtook her again.

When Angie woke up for the third time, the wooziness was gone.

The pain was not.

She forced her eyes open anyway and dealt with the familiar, horribly bright light. The chair was still at her side, and though Sam's clothes were different, he once again slept.

His jaw was dark, as if he hadn't shaved in a few days, and he looked so exhausted, so uncharacteristically ruffled, and so breathtaking she wanted to cry.

Then he stretched, lifted his head and saw her watching him. His eyes were no longer tired, but suddenly intent and solemn.

Then she no longer wanted to cry, she *was* crying. This is where he tells me he can't see me anymore, she thought.

She braced for the regret, the anger, but it didn't come. Yes, she'd fallen hard for him, but she'd done so with her eyes wide open. She'd do it again.

But this was going to hurt more than being shot. "Hi," she whispered.

"Hi," he whispered back.

A chair scraped the floor, and then another. Then a short gasp. Suddenly four additional heads appeared near Sam's.

Luke first, looking equally scruffy, but his eyes were twinkling with relief and a smile. "Hey, look at that. Sleeping Beauty is up."

Josephine's head popped into her vision next. "Oh, honey, you gave me gray hairs."

Then there were Angie's parents, looking at her as they always did—a little baffled, a little uncertain, but both clearly moved by the sight of her.

"You're going to be fine," her father said with his characteristic inability to deal with things going any other way.

"Of course she is," her mother said, as always in complete agreement with her father, unless of course, his opinion differed from her own, which only happened every other moment. "And you're going to be quick about it. You have things to do."

In other words, she had a life to make something of. While that might have felt like a burden in her past, it no longer felt like anything other than a wonderful challenge she couldn't wait to get back to.

Sam was still staring down at her, silent. Which reminded her…the life she couldn't wait to get back to…it wasn't always going to be a bowl of cherries.

The real world, *her* world, was still going to include things like…pain. She would miss him so much. So very much. "I don't remember how I got here."

"Ambulance," Luke said. "You didn't hear our hero here bellowing at the paramedic?"

Sam shot Luke a warning look. "She doesn't need details."

"Sure she does." Luke sat at her hip and grinned. "He nearly gave the poor medic a heart attack."

"Really?" Angie looked at Sam, fascinated by the fact that he was squirming.

"He had to be forcibly torn from your side," Luke said.

"This wasn't your fault," Angie told Sam.

"I know."

Luke put a finger in his ear and wriggled. "Oh really? You know, huh? Then why have you been barking at me for three days?"

"Because you're an idiot."

"Because you've been afraid. Which I understood. It's why I let you yell at me. You think I do that for just anyone?" Luke leaned closer to Angie.

"All that putting up with him while you've been resting…I probably deserve a kiss. You know, to help soothe my hurt feelings."

Angie smiled and kissed his cheek when he bent and put it in front of her.

Sam shoved Luke clear. "Go kiss your own woman." He turned back to Angie, his eyes dark with things she couldn't even imagine. "You really don't remember any of it? The surgery?"

"Surgery?" She swallowed. "No."

"You had the bullet lodged beneath your collarbone. It ricocheted around a bit, did some damage."

"Missed a few important parts by the skin of your teeth," Josephine said, biting her lower lip. Sam tossed her a dark look. "Not that you need to worry about that right now," she added quickly. "You're going to be fine, just fine. You'll be back in working order in no time at all."

The pain in her body made her think it might take slightly more time than no time. "I hope I can get back to work soon."

"Don't worry about work," Sam said.

"I'll get a temp, honey, no problem."

But living without money coming in would be a problem. A big one. And yet with everyone looking at her anxiously behind huge smiles, she didn't have the heart to say so.

Sam ran a finger down her arm to the IV, his jaw tight as he continued to gently stroke her. "Don't worry about work," he said again, softly.

Fine. She had plenty of other worries. Such as, how long before he put words to his feelings and walked away?

She wondered if she could pretend to go back to sleep to avoid that very thing. Wondered if he'd believe it. Wondered how long she could feign illness in order to delay what was so inevitable.

Something in her eyes must have given away her thoughts, because, without taking his eyes off her, he said, "Can we have a few moments here?"

A few moments would be bad. A few moments would be all he needed to tell her it was over, that what they'd shared had been a mistake. "I think I'd rather nap," she said hastily.

Worry filled his gaze. "You just woke up."

"We'll just get out of your hair for a bit." Luke leaned in so only Angie could hear him. "Keep him hopping, sweetie. It's good for him. *You're* good for him."

Wouldn't she like to believe that.

"You *are*," Luke said in the guise of kissing her.

"You're just what he needs. Not sure if he realizes that yet, but—"

"That's enough kissing," Sam said with some irritation.

Luke just grinned. "You can never have enough kissing."

Josephine pushed him away. She blew her nose noisily before looking Angie over very carefully. "It's good to see you, honey. So good. And yes, I imagine a nap would be just what the doctor ordered. You'll feel good as new in no time at all, I'm sure of it. Just holler if you need anything, okay? Anything at all."

Her parents came close next, and kissed her cheek. "We'll come back," her mother promised. "We can help. I could go get your class work for you, if you'd like."

"Really? Oh, Mom."

Her mother's eyes filled. "I'd do anything for you, Angie. I even finally understand you don't want to go to medical school." She smiled through the tears and kissed her again. "You're alive, and alive is good. I've decided everything else is a bonus. Sleep tight, sweetheart."

And then they too were gone.

Leaving Angie with Sam. Alone.

"Angie—"

She yawned, and didn't have to fake the heavy feeling to her lids. They were closing on her. "I'm so sleepy." Surely he wouldn't ditch her now, when she could hardly keep consciousness.

He could do it later, when she felt strong again. When she could stand on her own two feet and find her own balance. Then she'd be fine. She would.

"Just rest," he said quietly, keeping his hand on her, and she wasn't sorry for being selfish enough to want him to keep touching her for a few more stolen moments.

Just a few more.

As she let sleep claim her, she heard his sigh.

Sam had started to doze off himself when the hospital door opened again.

A nurse, probably needing to check Angie's stats.

Or maybe Luke with the promised pizza.

But it was neither. He lifted his head and faced... his mother.

"Hello, Sam," she said quietly, stepping farther into the room. She looked at Angie. "How is she?"

Sam couldn't seem to find his tongue. All these years...and she stood there in her sedate business suit holding a small sprig of flowers in her hands, looking as if they met like this on a daily basis. "Maybe I'm hallucinating from lack of sleep."

"No." She took a deep breath. "It's…me." She looked at the sleeping Angie. "It's all over the news. The nurse said she was going to be okay."

"She is." He cleared his throat. "What are you doing here? And how do you know Angie?"

"Well." She put the flowers down at the table by Angie's bed and lightly touched Angie's hand. Then she drew in another deep breath and faced her son. "She came into the library and set me straight on a few things."

"She…*what?*"

Now she let out that deep breath and came to Sam's side. Taking his hand, she pulled him to a stand, then slowly, very slowly, cupped his hard jaw. "I don't know where to start."

She was touching him. Looking at him with tears in her eyes and a world of hurt that he knew he'd put there. "The beginning, maybe?"

"Okay. The beginning." Her smile wobbled. "I was wrong to let you walk out of my life. Very, very wrong. I thought it would help if I couldn't watch you do what you do. But it's worse that way. I love you, Sam. You're my son."

"But I'm still a cop."

"Yes. And I'm still terrified over that, but not

enough to keep you out of my life. Not anymore. Please—" Her voice broke and she cleared her throat. "Please say you can find it in your heart to forgive me."

"But…why now?"

"Because life is too short," she said with surprising vehemence. "Too damn short." She dropped her gaze and backed away. "You probably have to think this over, and I understand. Just know whatever you decide, I'll understand that, too." She leaned forward, kissed him softly on the cheek and turned away.

Got to the door.

"Mom."

She whirled around, the hope on her face making his throat tighten—a chronic condition these days. "I…love you, too."

She put a shaking hand to her mouth. "Sam."

He opened his arms. And with a sob, she walked right into them.

Chapter 15

One week later, Angie left the hospital, arms over-flowing with flowers and get-well cards.

She left alone.

When the word had gone out that she'd be released, she'd received a strict message from Sam via one of the nurses. She was to wait until he got off work and he would drive her home.

She was to be coddled and cared for, apparently. But she didn't want that. She didn't want to be anyone's burden or responsibility, not ever again.

She'd found her strength.

Not that she hadn't appreciated the attention this week. It had been nice, reaffirming and incredibly touching to see how much everyone cared for her. She'd been ridiculously spoiled and, much to Sam's frustration, never alone.

Secretly she'd been relieved that he'd not managed to get her alone, because she couldn't possibly have maintained the smile she'd plastered on her face for long, the smile that said everything was just peachy.

It wasn't.

And he *had* tried to get her alone. In fact, the more he tried, the more frustrated he became, which greatly amused Luke whenever he stopped by.

It had become Angie's mission, cowardly as it was, to thwart Sam at every turn. She'd even convinced the doctor to release her earlier than planned, during a time she knew everyone would still be busy with their own lives. Especially Sam.

She left the hospital under her own steam. She would not be dumped while lying flat on her back, damn it.

A nurse ordered her a taxi, and when she got home, she stared at the front door and braced herself for the memories. Sam, and their first kiss. The break-in, and the subsequent terror. Not to mention the mess in her apartment she hadn't quite finished cleaning up, a mess she now knew had been created by Tommy Wilson, Ellie and George's son.

She still couldn't think of them without a stab of pain at their betrayal.

No more pity, she reminded herself firmly, keys in her hand, which shook only slightly.

The door creaked open as it always did, and childishly she slammed her eyes closed at the last second.

But she couldn't stand there on the porch all day. She felt weak from the effort it had taken to get this far. She hated that weakness.

By tomorrow she expected her body to be much more cooperative.

Knowing she had to, she slowly opened her eyes, but…there was no lingering mess, nothing out of place.

Even her plants had been repotted and the dirt vacuumed away.

Who would have done such a thing? Josephine didn't have a key to her place. Her parents had a spare, but they'd never let themselves in, had never even come over except when she'd first moved in.

She wandered through, marveling at all the work. Even her clothes had been picked up. *Folded.*

And then she saw her kitchen table, and the box of unopened paints on top of a large pad of artist's paper.

No note, but none was needed. Chest tight, she moved closer, touching the beautiful, new colors.

There was only one person who'd know to buy her such a gift. Only one person who would come to her apartment and make sure everything was cleaned up to spare her feelings, her memories.

Sam.

Her eyes welled and she sniffed loudly, deciding she could indulge in one last emotional moment. But suddenly, she felt bone-deep tired. She sank to a chair at the table and stared at the new things. What she'd give for the energy to dig right in and lose herself in her artwork.

Later.

Because right now she felt like putting her head on her arms and just…falling asleep.

Sam found her like that, and at the sight his heart broke a little.

Her sweater had fallen off one shoulder. Beneath the thin T-shirt she wore were the bandages on her shoulder and torso, and his gut clenched as it had every single time he'd looked at her since she'd been shot. Since she'd nearly died in his arms.

Why hadn't she waited for him at the hospital? Why had she come home alone?

Earlier he'd come with a cleaning crew to her

apartment, had helped them put the place back together, so that she wouldn't have to.

Then he'd gone to work for a while to face the mountain of paperwork waiting for him, but that hadn't kept his attention for long. Nothing kept his attention long these days.

Except Angie.

Soon as he could, he'd gone to the hospital to bring her home. He'd planned on wooing her senseless with the paints and possibly a few of those mind-blowing kisses they always seemed to share, warming her up so that he could talk her into hearing what he had to say.

He knew she thought he wasn't capable of deep emotion. He knew he'd hurt her with his reaction when she'd said she'd loved him.

He knew she thought they were through.

And truthfully, he'd considered just that, for all of two seconds.

Bottom line, he couldn't live without her. He'd learned the hard way love wasn't easy. Love could be blind. Love could hurt.

But without it, life wasn't quite right. His life wasn't quite right without her.

Now all he had to do was tell her. Convince her he meant it.

But, God, she looked beat with the faint purple

smudges beneath her eyes and her entire body relaxed in a way that told him she was out for the count. She probably hadn't slept decently at the hospital, and needed nothing but rest. Alone.

He'd gotten that message clear enough when he'd gone to the hospital and found an empty bed. That had nearly given him heart failure, until a nurse had told him she'd taken a cab.

Yes, she'd gotten his message, the nurse had assured him. And yes, she'd left anyway.

Leaning down, he softly brushed his lips against her cheek. She didn't so much as twitch, not even when he ran a hand down her hair, over her slim back. Exhaustion, poor baby. Careful not to touch her bandages, he lifted her up against his chest.

She let out a little protesting murmur.

"Shh," he whispered, his lips just below her ear. She felt so small, so vulnerable, and his gut clenched again, hard. "Just me."

"I'm tired," she said, eyes still closed.

"You need more sleep."

"I'm not really up for company." But she snaked her arms around his neck and held on tight.

"I'm not company."

"Hmm." She put her face to his throat. "Then what are you?"

He'd started walking with her, down the hallway, and stopped in the doorway to her bedroom.

What was he?

He knew what he wanted to be. "Why didn't you wait for me? I wanted to take you home."

"I wanted to come home by myself." She still hadn't opened her eyes, but her fingers were playing with the sensitive skin at the back of his neck, twining in his hair. "The cleaning up. The paints. It's all very sweet." Now she opened those dark, gorgeous eyes and laid them right on him. "Thank you. But I'm not going to forget how to live, if that's what you were worried about. I'm going to be fine."

"Yes." His voice was hoarse and he cleared it. "I think you are."

But would he? Now *that* was the question.

She looked at the bed. "And I could have walked here."

His hands tightened on her. "I felt like carrying you."

"Thank you," she said politely, clearly expecting him to set her down. Expecting him to walk away.

With her still in his arms, he sat on the bed and scooted back so he leaned against the headboard.

"You can let me go now. I won't break." Her smile was sad. "I'm much stronger than I look."

"Yes, but I'm not."

"What? You're the strongest person I know."

Leaning down, he put his lips very gently to hers. "I'm stronger when I'm with you."

"Sam." She licked her dry lips and searched his gaze. "That doesn't make any sense."

"Did you know my heart stopped when you got shot?"

When her eyes filled, with one lone tear escaping, he cupped her face and used his thumb to swipe it away. "I didn't tell you that to make you cry."

"You worried. I'm sorry."

"I don't want you to be sorry. I want you whole and healthy. I want the nightmare to never have happened. When I think how close I came to losing you…" Now his own eyes burned and he closed them for a long moment before opening them and touching his forehead to hers. "I was afraid you would die, and I'd been too selfish to share myself with you."

"Share what?"

"Me. My heart. Everything. God, Angie… you've brought me so much, everything that was missing in my life."

"What was missing in your life?"

"Love. I love you, Angie."

Now she cupped his face, too, and used her fingers to stroke his jaw. "It's the adrenaline talking," she whispered. "You're…" Her voice hitched. "You're saying this because of what happened to me. That's all."

"I'm saying it because it's true."

At her look of disbelief, he let out a disparaging sound. "Okay, maybe it took watching the blood drain out of you to know exactly how my life would be over if you weren't in it, but I knew I loved you before. If you want the truth, I knew I was going to love you from that very first day when you sat on that cold bank floor in my arms, blinking and squinting without your glasses, looking at me as if I was the only person in your life that mattered."

She wasn't wearing her glasses now, either, and she blinked and squinted up into his face. "You *are* the only person that matters."

His throat closed, simply closed.

"I thought you knew that by now."

Slowly he nodded. "I think it's beginning to sink in. When you look at me like that…I feel like a superhero. I can do anything, be anything. Say you still love me, Angie. Say I'm not too late. Say you'll marry me and give me the rest of your life."

Angie looked at him for a long, long moment, with her entire heart in her eyes.

Hope fed him. But then she slowly, ever so slowly, shook her head. "I'm sorry, Sam."

Chapter 16

Sam shook his head. "You're sorry."

"Yes." Angie was barely able to make her voice come out. "I'm…sorry."

"Usually when a man asks a woman to marry him, she says yes or no." He looked utterly bewildered. "I guess I didn't expect an 'I'm sorry.'"

Talking past the lump in her throat wasn't easy. Neither was looking into his eyes now filled with wariness and hurt. "Sam." She took his hands, brought them to her chest, pressing them against the heart that loved him, the heart that would always love him. "I drive you crazy. Why would you want to marry me?"

"Because…" He seemed shocked she would ask. "You make me smile. You make me see things. You make me live." He lifted his shoulders and looked a little desperate. "And because I can't imagine doing any of that without you."

"I'm also too cheerful. A little naive. Ditzy sometimes— No, don't shake your head, I know what I am. All those things are alien to you, and sometimes…sometimes you look at me like I'm alien, too."

Sam closed his eyes and grimaced. "We've already established I'm an ass. Look, we're different, no doubt. But there's nothing wrong with a little variety in personalities."

"No," she agreed softly, her heart aching. "Variety is fine. But this is more than that. Sam, I love you with all my heart, but I can't—I won't—change, not even for you, the most wonderful man I've ever—"

He put his fingers to her lips, halting her words. "I love you, Angie. All of you—your joy, your exuberance, your everything, and I think I have all along. Yeah, you scared the hell out of me, no doubt, but only because I wasn't ready for you."

"And you are now?"

"I am now," he said in a voice of steel, the one that told her he meant it and that he would never change his mind. "I trust you with all the things I never wanted to trust anyone with ever again—my emotions, my heart. My soul." He managed a smile. "Be kind to them," he whispered, stroking her cheek. "Be kind and say yes."

Her eyes filled. "Oh, Sam." She wrapped her arms around him.

He buried his face in her hair. "Is that a yes?"

"Yes." She laughed and cried at the same time. "Yes, I want it all. To be your wife, your heart. I can't think of anything I want more." Pulling back, she kissed him long and deep. "Except maybe your children."

"Angie." He stared at her, his hands on her hips to hold her close. "You're not…?"

"No." She kissed him again and slid her body against his until she felt his body respond. "But I want to be." She straddled him and let out a hum of pleasure at what she felt nudging between her thighs.

"Your shoulder. Careful—" He broke off with a low groan when she rocked against him. "Angie."

"Not all my parts hurt," she said a little wickedly, making him laugh now even as he groaned again. "Are you really going to love me, Sam?" She nibbled at his neck, thrilling to his rough groan, loving the power of making this strong man weak.

"And give me everything I've ever wanted? For the rest of my life?"

"Yes. Everything. A house. A new car. Your education. Whatever you want."

She smiled, feeling her heart lighten for the first time in…well, ever. "Those things are nice. But all I want is you. Haven't you figured that out yet?"

He went still as stone, his eyes suspiciously bright. Then he kissed her, and by the wondrous feelings it invoked, she knew he'd put everything he had into that kiss.

Lifting her head, she sighed, so full of love she could burst. "This is really going to work, isn't it? The cop and the waitress?"

"No doubt in my mind."

"Well, then." She hugged him tight. "This is going to be the best happy-ever-after there ever was."

"No doubt in my mind," he repeated softly.

Then he carefully laid her back on the bed and followed her down.

Epilogue

Four years later

Angie walked down the hallway of the police station, smiling and waving at all the people who'd become her friends over the years.

An arm snaked around her waist from behind, and she was swung about for a big bear hug.

"When are you going to leave that no-good husband of yours and marry me?" came a growl in her ear.

Angie pulled back to kiss Luke on the cheek. "What do you think the single-women population would say to that?"

"'Thank you.'"

Angie laughed. "Are you kidding? They'd mourn for days. Months."

"Years?" Luke asked hopefully.

Angie laughed again and pushed him aside with her free hand. In the other, she held a present. It was a small one, wrapped with a pink ribbon, which, she reflected, might be a dead giveaway, but she hadn't been able to resist. "Where's Sam?"

"Buried under paperwork. I hope you brought something to lighten the mood around here." He hopefully eyed the present. "Is that chocolate?"

"Sorry." In front of Sam's office door, she stopped and put a hand to her racing heart. They'd been waiting for so long, and now, after four years of college and her summer internship at a local museum, she was finally set in a job she loved, teaching children about art.

She was finally ready.

She hoped he was.

Slowly she opened the door, her heart leaping anew when Sam looked up. At the sight of her, he brightened.

"Hey, baby." Rising, he came around his desk and hauled her close. "What are you doing here so early? I thought you were busy training at the museum."

"I was." Nerves leaping, she thrust out the package.

Sam smiled and rubbed his flat belly. "Chocolate? Good, I'm starved."

"It's...not food."

"Hmm," he said, perplexed, undoing the ribbon without a care as she knew he would, opening the box and pulling out... "A piece of paper?" His frown turned to a horrified scowl. "From Dr. Kennedy?" His intense gaze met hers. "This is a blood test. Yours."

"Yes, I—"

"Angie?" He gripped her shoulders, backed her to a chair. Pale now, he hunkered at her side and cupped her face. "What's the matter?"

"Well..." She set her hands on his wrists and managed a shaky smile. "This is silly, isn't it? I didn't think it would be so hard to say out loud. I mean we talked about it, but neither of us had the greatest experience growing up, and—"

"Angie." He skimmed the report, swallowed hard and looked back up at her. "You're..."

With his hand in hers, she set it low on her stomach. "Yes. I'm..." She grinned. "Do you think either of us will ever be able to say it?"

He whooped, surged to his feet and twirled her around all in one smooth motion. Then he gently set her on her feet and put his forehead to hers. "We're going to be good at this."

She put her hands on his jaw and smiled. "Yes. I think we are."

"You should sit down."

Angie laughed. "There will be plenty of time for that in the coming months."

"Are you saying our little child is going to be a handful?"

"I'm sure of it."

Sam stared at her. "Maybe *I* should sit down."

She laughed. And in the end, they both sat down, Sam first, Angie in his lap, in his arms…right where she wanted to be, forever.

* * * * *

Fall in Love with...

MEN
in UNIFORM

YES! Please send me the exciting *Men in Uniform* collection. This collection will begin with 3 FREE BOOKS and 2 FREE GIFTS in my very first shipment—and more valuable free gifts will follow! My books will arrive in 8 monthly shipments until I have the entire 51-book *Men in Uniform* collection. I will receive 2 free books in each shipment and I will pay just $4.49 U.S./$5.39 CDN for each of the other 4 books in each shipment, plus $2.99 for shipping and handling.* If I decide to keep the entire collection, I'll only have paid for 32 books because 19 books are free. I understand that accepting the 3 free books and gifts places me under no obligation to buy anything. I can always return a shipment and cancel at any time. My free books and gifts are mine to keep no matter what I decide.

263 HDK 2653   463 HDK 2653

Name	(PLEASE PRINT)

Address	Apt. #

City	State/Prov.	Zip/Postal Code

Signature (if under 18, a parent or guardian must sign)

Mail to the **Harlequin Reader Service:**
IN U.S.A.: P.O. Box 1867, Buffalo, NY 14240-1867
IN CANADA: P.O. Box 609, Fort Erie, Ontario L2A 5X3

* Terms and prices subject to change without notice. Prices do not include applicable taxes. Sales tax applicable in N.Y. Canadian residents will be charged applicable taxes. This offer is limited to one order per household. All orders subject to approval. Credit or debit balances in a customer's account(s) may be offset by any other outstanding balance owed by or to the customer. Please allow 4–6 weeks for delivery. Offer available while quantities last. Offer not available to Quebec residents.

Your privacy: Harlequin is committed to protecting your privacy. Our Privacy Policy is available online at www.eHarlequin.com or upon request from the Reader Service. From time to time we may make our lists of customers available to reputable third parties who have a product or service of interest to you. If you would prefer we not share your name and address, please check here. ☐

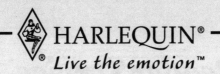